Kate flopped back

Way to go. Nothing like a bloodcurdling
scream to waylay suspicion. No telling what
Cole thought she had in her closet now. Drugs.
Stolen jewelry. A bag full of cash.

She got out of bed and opened the closet,
feeling around for the leather case. Still there.

She pulled out the suitcase, opened it and
stared down at the neatly stacked rows of bills.
A little over one million dollars. By rights, it
was hers. Karl had stolen every cent of it. Left
her virtually penniless.

So getting this money back meant she had
beaten her ex-husband at his own game. In the
end, she'd won.

She should be drinking champagne.
Celebrating.

She went to the sink and stared at herself
in the small mirror. But what was there to
celebrate, really? She'd regained a few strands
of her tattered pride. So what? It didn't change
the fact that she was thirty-three years old, had
never worked a day in her far-too-cushioned
life and had no idea where to go from here.

Dear Reader,

A Woman with Secrets was a fun story to write. I love the Caribbean and have always thought it would be great to sail around for a while, island to island, living like someone content to leave all memories of fifteen-degree winter mornings in the been-there-done-that file.

On arriving in Miami for a ten-day excursion of just this sort, Kate Winthrop gets both more and less than she'd bargained for. When the story starts, she is completely absorbed with the need to exact revenge on an ex-husband. But aboard the *Ginny*, Kate finds herself falling in love with Cole Hunter, and she begins to see that she can be someone she never imagined she could be. By the end of the trip, Kate has let go of her need for revenge and is motivated to make her once-shallow life mean something.

While I hope *A Woman with Secrets* has its moments of humor and lightheartedness, I found myself unable to resist weaving threads of seriousness through the story. Maybe this is a reflection of my increasing awareness of a need to look outside myself to those situations where even a small effort on my part can make a difference to another living being. The ripple effect of kindness continues to amaze me. When people link hands and take it upon themselves to make a difference, incredible things can be done.

I like to think this is the place where Kate is at the end of *A Woman with Secrets*. A place where happiness is a direct result of giving instead of taking.

I love to hear from readers. Please write to me at P.O. Box 973, Rocky Mount, VA 24151. E-mail at inglathc@aol.com. Or visit my Web site at www.inglathcooper.com.

All best,

Inglath

A WOMAN WITH SECRETS

Inglath Cooper

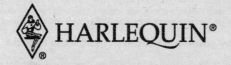

HARLEQUIN®

TORONTO • NEW YORK • LONDON
AMSTERDAM • PARIS • SYDNEY • HAMBURG
STOCKHOLM • ATHENS • TOKYO • MILAN • MADRID
PRAGUE • WARSAW • BUDAPEST • AUCKLAND

ISBN-13: 978-0-373-71384-4
ISBN-10:   0-373-71384-3

A WOMAN WITH SECRETS

www.eHarlequin.com

Printed in U.S.A.

ABOUT THE AUTHOR

Inglath Cooper is a RITA® Award-winning author of seven published novels. Her books focus on the dynamics of relationships—those between a man and a woman, mother and daughter, sisters, friends. Her stories are often peopled with characters who reflect the values and traditions of the small Virginia town where she grew up.

Books by Inglath Cooper

HARLEQUIN SUPERROMANCE

SIGNATURE SELECT

Don't miss any of our special offers. Write to us at the following address for information on our newest releases.

Harlequin Reader Service
U.S.: 3010 Walden Ave., P.O. Box 1325, Buffalo, NY 14269
Canadian: P.O. Box 609, Fort Erie, Ont. L2A 5X3

To my Dad, for showing me the true definition of courage and determination.

And to my editor, Johanna Raisanen, for being such an absolute pleasure to work with. An eye for story weaknesses, a kind manner and she loves dogs, too. Need I say more?

CHAPTER ONE

Even a dog knows the difference between being stumbled over and being kicked.
—American Proverb

KATE WINTHROP HAD REACHED an all-time low. She was broke. Desperate. And about to become a thief.

She had her ex-husband to thank for each of these mantles. And if it were the last thing she did on God's green earth, she planned to get even with him.

She made this resolution in the backyard of the castle-size Georgian house Karl had recently purchased in one of Richmond's more lavish neighborhoods. Amazing in itself, considering he supposedly had no money. But then, he had her money, and it didn't look as though either conscience or good sense had prevented him from spending it.

A car drove by, the lights arcing across the

backyard, catching her in its glare for a flash of a second. She stepped back into the shadows, her heart relocating in her throat. She waited a full minute after the car had passed before peeling herself off the brick wall.

A headline flashed in front of her: Kate Winthrop, Daughter of Self-made Millionaire Hart Winthrop, Five to Ten in State Pen.

Long headline, but point taken.

She knew it was crazy, coming here like this. Even so, she could no more make herself leave than she could erase the mental image of Karl stealing her blind day by day, week by week for the past three years. As it always did, the thought brought with it fresh humiliation.

She stepped back and studied the house. Karl lived by the creed that more was more. Here, that principle had been put to adequate test.

A pool took up most of the suburban backyard, surrounded by expensive, imported planters that anchored boxwoods the size of an overfed sumo wrestler. Wrought-iron loungers with plump cushions sat in neat rows at the water's edge.

She pictured herself upending each of them into the blue water. That was too petty, though. She was here for real evidence. Something concrete. Something she could take to the police, wave in their faces with an indignant, "See, I told you he was a scumbag!"

As to what that would be, she had no idea. She'd know it when she saw it. In all reality, could someone really embezzle millions of dollars without leaving a trail of some sort?

She patted a hand against the pocket of her zip-up vest and pulled out her flashlight. She glanced down at the rest of her outfit. Turtleneck, gloves, cargo pants, boots. So maybe she'd gotten a little carried away with the *Mission Impossible* theme.

French doors served as a wall to the back of the house. She stepped forward and pressed her face against the glass, peering into the darkened living room. After learning that Karl and his new wife would be out of town until tomorrow afternoon, Kate had called the house earlier in the day to inform the maid she had a package to deliver to Mr. Forrester. Berta—leave it to Karl to import a German housekeeper—had said she would be there until 6:00 p.m. It was now seven-thirty. All the lights were off in the house, no one home. Still, her stomach dropped at the thought of being caught.

But then she envisioned herself standing in front of the divorce court judge, heard him say that as far as he could see, she had knowingly and willingly given her husband the authority to do with their joint funds as he had seen fit. "His name is on all the accounts, dear," he'd said, Southern disdain for her idiocy marking each word. "Your husband might have made some bad decisions, but there's no law against that. I suggest you be careful who you marry next time, young lady."

So there was no law against robbing your wife blind. There was, however, a law against breaking and entering. She sent a quick glance over both shoulders, then turned the flashlight around and placed the butt of it against the glass pane nearest the door handle. A quick jab, and the glass shattered, falling to the floor on the other side. She reached through the open cavity and pressed the lock. The door swung open, and the silence exploded.

She jumped as if poked with a cattle prod, even though she'd fully expected an extra-loud alarm system. Extra was Karl's style. If you could super-size it, his name was on the dotted line.

She stepped inside and closed the door, using the flashlight to wind her way down the hall to the front of the house.

The control panel was where she'd thought it would be: to the left of the door. She had forty-five seconds to figure out the code and turn off the alarm before the security company called. Earlier that day, she'd invested a couple of hours in coming up with the combinations Karl might have used.

Being married to Karl had left her with an absolute understanding of the three engines that pulled his train of thought: golf, women and money. And not necessarily in that order.

From her pants pocket, she pulled the piece of paper on which she'd written her best guesses.

First, golf. With one gloved finger, she punched in the two scores he had bragged about so often that the numbers were seared in her brain. 6265.

But the ear-piercing wail continued.

Door number two: women. She punched in 3624, picturing Karl's wife—Tiffany-the-interior-decorator, her surgically enhanced figure leaving little doubt as to what had initiated his defection.

But clearly Karl had not immortalized Tiffany's measurements in his alarm control panel. It continued its wail. Her nerve endings were beginning to feel as if they'd been dipped in Tabasco Sauce.

One more. Time was running out. She had ten seconds max. Next on the list: Karl's penchant for picking stocks. He played the market the way little old ladies in Las Vegas played the quarter slot machines, going online ten or fifteen times a day to monitor his latest picks. He'd hit the jackpot once, quoting the stock's sell price to anyone who would listen. She glanced at the piece of notepaper on which she'd written the last of her three guesses.

What if she were wrong?

She drew in a deep, hopeful breath and punched in the numbers.

The wailing immediately ceased. Ah. Silence. Peaceful, blessed silence.

And then she grew indignant again. It figured, after all. When it came right down to it, everything that mattered most to Karl centered around money. Without it, he couldn't afford golf or women.

She leaned her head against the wall, gathering up her now shredded nerves of steel. A neighbor could have heard the alarm. The police could be on their way right this minute.

Even as she indulged her paranoia, she knew the closest house lay well out of earshot. It wasn't likely that the police would have been notified. Now that the alarm was off, she should have all night to search the house.

Still slumping with relief, she turned around and waved the flashlight across the room. The main living area looked like a candy cane factory, the red-and-white stripes on the walls nearly blinding her. A hysterical giggle bubbled up from her throat and broke free, the sound ridiculous in the otherwise tomb-still house. Appearances were important to

Karl. She wondered if he provided his business associates with protective eyewear when he entertained here.

She left the vertigo-inducing living room and aimed the flashlight down the hallway that led to the rest of the house. Tiffany's touch had found its way to these walls as well. Karl now had stripes in black and white, green and white, pink and white. The upside? If she could find something to convince the police he was a crook, he'd have no problem adjusting to his prison uniform.

The house felt eerie, pitch black as it was. But she didn't dare turn on any lights for fear that someone would notice and report it. Like the alarm code, she had planned this part of her efforts as well. She'd start with the most obvious place: Karl's office. Using the flashlight as a guide, she poked her head inside several different rooms until she found it.

Here, Tiffany had given up the striped wallpaper for paint. Purple was her color of choice, although Kate would bet Karl had dubbed it eggplant.

She headed for the desk, sat down in Karl's leather chair and began opening drawers, using the flashlight to illuminate their contents. The first three yielded nothing more than paper clips and files full of papers that meant nothing to her.

The bottom drawer was locked.

But she'd come prepared for locked drawers. She reached inside her vest pocket and pulled out the small black case that held a series of lock picks she'd managed to purchase at a pawn shop in the seedier part of Richmond.

She chose one and got to work, fumbling at first, then getting the hang of it. The first four did nothing. The fifth one, however, did the trick.

The drawer popped open. Again, there were files, neatly organized. Behind them sat a metal box. She reached for it first, surprised to find it unlocked. She popped the latch and then sat a little straighter at the sight of the gun nestled inside. What was Karl doing with a gun? A big one at that. In three years of marriage, she'd never known he had one.

Maybe he and Tiffany played games with it. A mental picture she didn't need.

Glad she'd reached the point where she could actually joke about the biggest mistake of her life, she slammed the lid closed and stuck the box back in the drawer. She worked on the files then, leafing through each of them in the hope that something incriminating would jump out at her.

Nothing did.

Twenty minutes later, she'd found little more than

records of car loans, garage services, health insurance.

She slumped in the chair, her ponytail squished against the cushioned back. There had to be something in this mausoleum of a house to prove what a lying, cheating...

She put the brakes on that particular rant. It was old territory, after all. Trekked across one too many times.

Looking back, she could see everything so clearly now. Not that it did her any good to have such remarkable hindsight—a worthless commodity, after all.

With renewed determination, she got up from the chair and headed for the master bedroom, where lace and mirrors were the key decorating ingredients. She wondered where Tiffany had actually managed to get her hands on an interior design degree. The house was an aesthetic assault to the senses.

She started with the nightstands by the bed, emptying the contents of their drawers on top of the black duvet. She shook her head. Black? Really.

She rifled through hand lotion, Chap Stick, a few receipts, theater ticket stubs. She worked her way through each drawer in the room, ending up in an enormous walk-in closet that could easily double as a retail store. She closed the door and flipped on the light switch. She patted down every suit, looked under every sweater, opened every shoe box.

Nothing.

She sank onto the floor and dropped her head in her hands. Maybe it was time to accept the fact that she had been used. That she'd let herself be conned by a man who planned her fleecing down to the last dime. Maybe it was time to put it all behind her and start over again. At McDonald's, maybe. Polyester uniforms could do a lot for a girl with natural curves. Emphasis on natural.

She got to her feet and glanced at her watch. Time to admit defeat. She gave one of Karl's Ferragamo loafers a kick and sent it hurtling across the floor. It landed against the baseboard of the closet with a loud whack.

She stared at it for a moment. Was the board loose, or was her desperation making her see things?

She got down on her knees and poked it with an index finger. The baseboard moved. She shoved the shoe aside and gave the board a tug. It loosened easily.

Renewed hope tumbled through her like a shot of straight adrenaline. Pressing her left ear to the floor, she peered into the hole, then stuck her hand in, encountering something hard.

She fumbled for the flashlight, and then beaming it into the hole, spotted what looked like a leather bag.

Heart pounding, she dropped onto the carpet, planted one foot on either side of the opening, then grabbed the bottom of the exposed wall with both hands and pulled. It gave, and a small section of the wall opened up like the entrance to Aladdin's cave.

She sat there for a stunned second or two. Then she reached out and eased the bag forward. She popped the latches and it opened. She froze.

Money. Stacks and stacks of it. She picked up a bundle and fanned the edges. All one hundred dollar bills. Too many to count.

She sat for a long time, not moving, just staring at what she'd found, the taste of revenge sweet on her tongue even as she reached a whole new level of understanding about her husband's betrayal.

She tilted the satchel up and emptied its contents onto the floor. There had to be at least a million dollars. Maybe more.

So what now?

If she left this house with the money, Karl would be hot on her heels as soon as he discovered it missing.

But what could he do? Go to the police and accuse her of stealing back what was hers to begin with? Let him try. Stupid, once, yes. Next time, he would find her a worthy opponent.

She waited until she'd arrived back at her

apartment before she called Tyler Bennett's home number. He'd worked for her father for years and represented Kate in her divorce from Karl as well. After three rings, he answered with an indignant hello.

"It's Kate," she said. "Sorry to call so late."

A fumbling sound was followed by, "It's the middle of the night."

"I know. You'll be happy to hear I can now be removed from your delinquent accounts list."

A big sigh, and then he said, "You called to tell me this?"

"I thought you'd be pleased."

"You want to tell me what this is really about?"

"You won't approve."

"Kate, didn't I tell you to stay away from Karl?"

"You did, yes. Which I agree, under normal circumstances, is very good advice. It just so happens he separated himself from a good portion of my money long enough for me to find it." She glanced at the pile of money on her bed and smiled.

The ensuing stretch of silence made her wonder if he had fallen back to sleep. "I realize your fondest dream is to put Karl in jail," he said in a careful voice. "But as your attorney, I have to tell you this kind of behavior is going to land *you* behind bars."

"For taking back what was mine to begin

with?" she asked, unable to keep the indignation from her voice.

"There are ways to handle these things, Kate. This is not one of them."

"Yes, I've had a relatively good indoctrination to the legal way."

"And what do you think he's going to do when he finds the money missing?"

"I'd love to be there to see it, but I think I'll forego the pleasure and give him a little time to cool off. In fact, that's why I'm calling. You and Peg are leaving for a cruise day after tomorrow, right? She mentioned a buddy of yours from law school runs the tours."

"Yeah," Tyler said cautiously.

"How much would you take for those tickets?" she asked.

A full fifteen minutes later, she had finally convinced him to sell her the tickets. Although he made a valiant effort to convince her she might be stepping off the ledge of sanity.

"I'll pick them up at your office first thing in the morning," she said and then hung up. She quickly stuffed the money back in the satchel, the thick shell of self-disgust she'd been wearing these past months melting under a wave of self-congratulation.

In finding Karl's stash, she had reversed the wheel of fortune. For a washed-up artist who'd been robbed of her demolished inheritance, it was a step in the right direction. Maybe Karl would be the one applying for a job at the Golden Arches.

She closed the latches on the leather bag and got to her feet. Paybacks were hell.

CHAPTER TWO

*It is a true saying that a man must eat a peck
of salt with his friend before he knows him.*
—Miguel de Cervantes Saavedra

COLE HUNTER RESTED AN ELBOW on the side of the
phone booth, the receiver tucked inside his left
shoulder, his gaze fixed on the steamy pavement
beneath his feet. The Miami sun burned through the
back of his white T-shirt while barely suppressed
frustration bucked inside him.

"Look, Sam, no insult intended here," he said,
struggling to keep his voice even, while barely
restraining the urge to shout, "but why should I
believe you're any closer to finding my daughter
now than you were all the other times?"

"I know I've told you I was close before,"
Sam said, his diplomacy failing to coat Cole's ir-
ritation, "but I've managed to connect with a

discarded boyfriend of your ex-wife. Apparently, she dumped him, and he's not too happy with her."

Cole had no trouble believing this. Casting people aside, after all, was Pamela's forte. "And he said he knows where she is?" he asked, trying not to let himself get too hopeful.

Lately, he'd begun to think he would never see Ginny again. And in a way, it had become easier to let himself believe that than to believe in something that might never actually happen.

"Said he does."

"And what does he want in return for that information?"

"Twenty thousand dollars."

"Then give it to him," Cole said without hesitation, glad for once of the investments he'd made early in his law career, the returns on which he now lived. "I'll make a transfer to your account as soon as we hang up."

"Done. But I'll have to wait for him to call me."

"Are you telling me you can't get in touch with him?" he asked, incredulous.

"That's the way the guy wanted it."

Disbelief blasted through Cole, skepticism fast on its heels. "Are you sure he's on the up and up?"

"He insisted on playing things his way. Look,

Cole, I know how anxious you are to find your daughter," the detective said, "but you've waited this long. Don't give up now. I have a really good feeling about this lead."

Cole wanted to believe him. And what choice did he have but to go along? If this Pamela castoff could help locate Ginny, then Cole could stomach the idea of doing it his way. "I'll be going out for the next ten days this afternoon," he said. "You have the numbers to reach me. The reception's decent once I get out of port. Call as soon as you hear anything at all, okay?"

"Will do," Sam said and hung up.

Cole placed the receiver back on its hook, but didn't immediately let go. Some inner quirk of superstition kept his hand where it was, as if to sever the connection would also sever the possibility that he might actually find his daughter this time. It had been almost two years since he had seen Ginny. Nearly two years of wondering where she was. If she'd missed him. If she thought he was the one who'd abandoned her. The thought cut like a knife in his chest. To think his child might actually believe he didn't care about her, that he'd walked away from her...

Using his phone card, he dialed the number for his bank and made a transfer to Sam's account. He turned then and headed back down the boardwalk to the *Ginny*. A migraine loomed at the periphery of his vision like a hurricane off south Florida, hanging back and building up force.

Just short of his boat, he spotted Harry Smith spread-eagled across the bow, adding another layer to his suntan. The pounding in his temples gained momentum.

Harry showed up with predictable frequency, usually accompanied by a couple of string-bean-thin blondes, one of which he always offered to Cole—generous guy that he was—despite the fact that he had yet to take him up on his offerings.

Harry raised his head now and squinted in Cole's direction. "The love boat's back in port," he said, getting up and jumping onto the dock, his smile chastising. "And it's a wonder, after you all but sank it."

Cole shot him a look. "You're the one who can't function without a woman on each arm. I'm managing just fine."

Harry hailed from Savannah and everything about him suggested old money. At thirty-six, he thoroughly enjoyed his reputation as a playboy and did whatever he could to further it. Heir apparent to a silver fortune, he spent his days cruising around the Caribbean on his father's yacht, his deck decorated with sun-adoring women who were drawn to him like honeybees to ice cream.

"Unlike you," Harry said, "I'm not cursed with an aversion to the female gender. You're the one living like a monk. Don't you think there's a little something wrong with a guy who never takes advantage of the fruit just waitin' to be picked off the trees?"

"Have you ever noticed how fruit can be fresh one day and rotten the next?" Cole asked.

Harry rolled this around a moment, and then said, "You know, you should move to Alaska. They wear parkas there instead of bikinis."

"It's a thought," he agreed, refusing to rise to the bait. He had to give Harry credit for tenacity. Harry couldn't understand how any red-blooded male could survive two years without a woman. As someone with skid marks on his heart, Cole wasn't real keen to repeat the experience. The only thing he cared about was getting his daughter back and making sure Pamela never saw her again. As for the rest of his life, he was just biding time.

"You see, Cole," Harry said, "you're not playing the game by the right rules. Nobody said you've got to fall in love. I walked that plank once myself, and if anybody knows there are sharks below, I do. This is all about fun. Nothing more. Nothing less."

"You really buy that crap?" he asked, amused.

"Sure I do."

Cole shook his head. "Somebody always wants more, Harry. That, you can count on."

"Fine, fine," he said. "But next time you get lonely for a little female companionship, don't come looking for—"

"I won't." He picked up the bottle of water sitting by the rail of the boat and took a long draw on it. "What are you doing here, anyway? I thought you were going to be out for a while."

A shrug accompanied Harry's reply. "Met up with a little blond-haired gal who needed a lift."

"The Triple A of the Caribbean."

"I do what I can," Harry said with a slightly wicked grin.

"Excuse me."

The voice turned them both around. A woman stood on the dock, a pull-handle suitcase beside her, an expensive-looking leather satchel in her left hand. Harry's disgruntled expression disappeared behind an orthodontically correct smile.

"Can I help you with something, miss?" he asked with the charm that was part and parcel of his genetic code.

She glanced down at the sheet of paper in her hand and frowned. "This is Tracer Harbor, isn't it?"

Harry bolted forward as though a pot of scalding water had been tossed at his back. He took the paper from her hand, scanned its contents and shot Cole a rejuvenated grin. "Yes, ma'am. And this is the *Ginny*. Looks like you're in the right place."

The woman tipped her head and peered past them at the boat. "I— There's been some kind of a mistake, I'm afraid. I'm supposed to be booked on a cruise—"

"So you are," Harry squinted at the piece of paper, before saying, "Miss Winthrop. You're looking at the captain."

The woman's perfectly arched eyebrows drew together over a look of suspicion. "You're the captain?"

"Ah, no. I'm Harrison Smith. Friends call me Harry." Harry directed her gaze toward Cole, giving him a thumbs up signal behind her back. "Captain Cole Hunter, at your service. On that note, I have a few things to do. Down the dock," he said, pointing. "Over there. Well out of hearing range."

Ignoring Harry, Cole looked at the woman and said, "You're Tyler's friend?"

"Ah, yes. Kate Winthrop," she said. "Tyler spoke highly of your cruise." She shot a glance at the *Ginny*, then corrected herself. "Boat."

Cole had gone to law school with Tyler. He and

his wife Peg had been booked on the trip out of Miami today. He'd called and said they had a change of plans, but a friend would be taking their place. According to Tyler, this friend needed a vacation and wasn't opposed to a little roughing it.

Looking at her now, Cole strongly suspected roughing it for Ms. Winthrop meant getting booted from the Four Seasons to the Ritz-Carlton. She had that look. Diamond solitaires impressive enough to be her only jewelry. The kind of straight blond hair whose upkeep could probably support several mortgages. And blue jeans with designer holes in the knees.

"Passengers aren't supposed to arrive until later this afternoon," Cole said, glancing at the satchel she held in a death grip at her side.

"I've been driving for the past twenty hours," she said. "I thought maybe I'd be able to board early." She glanced at the boat behind him, crestfallen, as if she'd been anticipating a version of the *QEII* and had just realized she was getting a tugboat.

"Tyler did tell you this is a working vacation, didn't he?"

She shifted from one foot to the other. "Working vacation? No, I just assumed—"

"Look, Ms. Winthrop, there's nothing fancy about what you've signed on for," he interrupted, his patience waning. "Everyone is expected to do his or her part whether it's helping out in the kitchen or fishing for dinner. I have one crew member, but the idea is it's pretty much your boat for the duration."

She blinked hard, her grip on the satchel tightening. "But I...don't know anything about boats."

He bit back a sigh. Before the day ended, the hurricane pounding at his temples would no doubt hit land. He decided then and there that he would be far better off with a cancellation on his hands than taking Ms. Kate Winthrop on this excursion. Hitching a thumb back toward town, he said, "Try the Fontainebleau. It's a full-service hotel. Room service. Great big pool. The works. Much more your style, I'm sure."

THE WORDS RANG of insult.

Married to Karl for three years, Kate certainly knew one when she heard one.

Standing there in the bone-melting Florida heat, she stared at the back of the tall, sun-bronzed man now striding across the boardwalk toward his boat. Anger swelled inside her. Long overdue, without question. Life had landed her enough blows of late, and she had no intention of letting some overgrown Tom Sawyer with his shaggy hair, ragged cutoff jeans and bare feet change her plans.

Not that this was turning out at all as she had expected. She'd assumed the Bennetts' cruise plans would involve nothing more taxing than days spent by the pool sipping piña coladas. This particular vessel couldn't have been mistaken for a cruise ship in pitch dark and high seas.

But the likelihood of getting on a real ship at this late date was next to nil. And she wasn't about to let this boat sail without her. When Karl arrived back in Richmond, she intended to be somewhere in the middle of the ocean where he wouldn't stand the remotest chance of finding her.

"Captain Hunter!" she called out in the most humble voice she could muster.

He turned around, looking surprised to find her still standing there. "Was there something else I could do for you?" he asked.

She faltered under the set look on his face, cleared her throat, then said, "I'm not interested in a hotel. I'm booked for this cruise. I don't intend to change my plans."

He didn't say anything for several seconds, but merely stared at her as if she were a child for whom he had to find a convincing argument. "Look, Ms. Winthrop, you can't expect the rest of the group to carry your weight—"

"Captain Hunter," she interrupted, digging her

heels in. "I'm perfectly capable of taking care of myself. I don't expect anyone else to do it for me."

He watched her for several drawn out moments. Resisting the unfamiliar urge to fidget under his level gaze, she stood her ground. To her surprise, he let out a deep sigh and said, "Fine."

Relief whisked through her, followed quickly by a surge of indignation. Why did she care what he thought of her anyway? It wasn't as if he were what she'd expected. What had Tyler said about his old law school buddy? "Smart guy. *Summa cum laude* at Yale…"

This was what a *summa cum laude* from Yale did with his life? She'd assumed "running the cruise" meant from some skyscraper in New York City or wherever such types operated their investments. Not "running the boat," as in, sailing it, cleaning it, docking it.

And the man wasn't exactly dressed like the captain of a boat. His white T-shirt and cutoff jeans said Rebel with a capital *R*. So maybe he was handsome in a who-cares-what-the-rest-of-the-world-thinks sort of way. His dark blond hair had streaks of light in it. And his eyes were blue, like sea water.

She put a stop to her observations. She'd had enough of handsome men to last her a lifetime.

Karl had been handsome. *GQ.* Drop-dead. Turn-your-knees-to-water handsome. He was also a slug.

The man with the city-block-wide smile jogged back down the dock, his expression expectant when he called out, "You two get everything squared away?"

With his return came the realization that, unfortunately, she needed Cole Hunter and his less-than-cruiselike boat. Her disappearance would give Karl time to cool off and accept the fact that where their farcical and now dead marriage was concerned, she would be the one to have the last word. And she really, *really* wanted the last word. "Yes, I think so," she said.

Harry Smith sent a victory fist into the air. "Great. You don't know what you're in for, Miss Winthrop!"

She somehow suspected that he was right.

She waited while the two men held a huddle a few yards away, their voices low and hushed. Ignoring them, she stared off into the distance, concentrating on the sounds of sails snapping into line, laughter ringing from a yacht headed out of the harbor, a black French poodle barking from its guard post aboard an enormous catamaran.

The conversation behind her built to a crescendo. Harry Smith's voice carried a note of appeal, while Cole Hunter's rumbled resistance to whatever his friend was suggesting. Finally, the captain took the distance of the dock between them in a few swift strides, commandeering her two suitcases without saying a word. Her heart leapt into her throat. She shot after him, protesting, "That's all right. I can carry those."

But he kept walking, long, marked strides that said a good deal about his level of agitation. She slowed her pace and drew in a calming breath, reassuring herself that he had no idea what was inside the bag.

Even so, she frowned at his back. She didn't care if the man was Tyler's friend. He was rude. And she had a feeling that before this so-called vacation was over, she would tell him so.

She followed him down narrow stairs, through a doorway barely wider than her own body and into a cabin the size of a large closet.

"This is where you'll be staying," he said abruptly, plopping her two suitcases down by the bed.

With him in it, the room seemed Alice-in-Wonderland small. It was neat and clean though, the bed crisply made, the air tinted with the remnants of furniture polish.

"Anything you need?" he asked, obviously anxious to go.

"A pitcher of iced tea and a sandwich would be nice," she said, infusing the request with politeness.

His smile said *you're kidding right?*

Actually, she wasn't. She hadn't eaten in twelve hours. Something told her she should let this one go though.

"Dinner's at seven," he said and turned to leave.

"Captain Hunter?" she called out.

He ducked back inside the doorway with a look of restrained impatience. "Yes?"

"The other passengers. When will they be arriving?"

"Couple hours," he said.

"Oh. Good, then," she answered, reassured to know she wouldn't be sailing off alone into the sunset with Captain Grump and his sidekick.

After he left, she sank down on the bed, her stomach rumbling. Was she crazy? Maybe she should just get off the boat now. Maybe she should have stayed and confronted Karl. Taken the lizard to court and let him explain to a judge where the million dollars in his closet had come from. But she hadn't relished the idea of handing out a chunk of her father's already depleted funds in legal fees. Besides, Karl would need a little time to come to grips with the fact that he'd have to find some other means of financing Tiffany's decorating habit.

And, too, she told herself, spending the next ten days on a boat headed through the western

Caribbean could only be so bad. At least she wouldn't have to worry about Karl finding her. For now, at least, that was all she cared about.

FROM THE CORNER of the deck, Cole watched the lovely Ms. Winthrop struggle with the tarp he'd asked her to fold.

He could have done it himself. He hadn't needed to call her up from her cabin to do it, but he was holding out the hope that she'd change her mind and leave before the rest of the passengers arrived. He didn't have a good feeling about this woman.

Not to mention that Harry's matchmaking antennae had been on high alert since the moment he set eyes on her. He was certain God had finally taken pity on poor sex-starved Cole Hunter and sent him a woman no man could resist.

A breeze caught the end of the tarp and jerked one end of it from her grasp. Her dark navy pullover had started to cling to her arms and shoulders in wet patches. Sweat glistened on her forehead and upper lip. Several strands of blond hair had escaped the barrette at the back of her neck and stuck to her cheek.

He crossed the deck and reached for one end of the canvas. With a pointed look at her navy shirt, which now clung to her skin in some interesting places, he said, "By the way, dark colors draw the sun."

CHAPTER THREE

Man has a thousand plans, heaven but one.
—Chinese Proverb

CLEARLY, HE THOUGHT she was an idiot.

Folding a tarp. As though the boat would have sunk if she hadn't accomplished the task posthaste. She patted the final edge into place and managed an even reply, "Thanks for the tip."

"Don't mention it," he said.

From the other end of the dock came a lilting, "Yoo-hoo!"

Two older ladies with bluish, salon-set hair walked toward the boat, both wearing excited expressions. Behind them, a black-capped chauffeur wheeled a cartload of luggage. One of the women waved coral nails in their direction, the color picking up the floral background of her silk jumper. "Captain Hunter?"

He studied the two women through narrowed eyes. "Could I help you with something?"

"I certainly hope so. Is this the *Ginny?*"

He nodded once, answering reluctantly, "It is."

"Oh, good, Lily, we're in the right place," she said with an enthusiastic smile to the woman beside her.

"We're the Granger sisters," they said in unison.

Kate risked another look at Cole Hunter, whose set expression clearly indicated his passenger list was not turning out as he had expected.

She, on the other hand, was beginning to enjoy herself.

"I'm Lyle," the talkative one said. "And this is Lily."

The captain cleared his throat. "I thought you were…from your e-mail, I assumed you were husband and wife."

The quiet one said, "Oh, dear. We do confuse people don't we, Lyle?"

"Lily couldn't say Lyla as a child, and Lyle just stuck. I hope this won't make a difference with our accommodations. We expected to share a room. We're totally prepared for our share of tough living, Captain."

Kate watched with an undeniable stab of satisfaction as he eyed the mound of trunks being wheeled down the gangplank by the chauffeur. "Ladies, if you're planning to bring all that luggage, I'm afraid we have a problem."

"Oh. I suppose it is a tad much, isn't it?" Lily said, one finger to the side of her face. "But I can never decide what to bring, and Lyle thought we'd probably have room for it—"

"I'm afraid Lyle was wrong," he said grimly.

Lily's face fell. "Well, then—"

"Now, now, dear," Lyle said, patting her sister's shoulder. "You'll just have to eliminate a few things. No big deal, really."

At her reassurance, Lily brightened. "Of course, I will." She began instructing the chauffeur to open the trunks so that she might remove the most essential of items.

Essential appeared to include a glittering gold evening gown, black dinner suit and a pair of satin pumps. Obviously, Lyle and Lily hadn't been any more aware of the itinerary than Kate had.

Captain Hunter excused himself then, avoiding her gaze and telling the Granger sisters he'd be back as soon as he located some Aspirin.

While Lyle and Lily continued rummaging through their trunks, a man made his way down the gangplank. Somewhere near mid-fifties, his graying hair was slicked back in a past-era wet look. His bottle-thick glasses glinted in the sunlight. He wore a tweed jacket over a white shirt buttoned to the throat. A young woman, basically a female version of him, followed behind. She, too, wore a tweed jacket over a sensible cotton blouse and an equally sensible below-the-knee brown cotton skirt. Her eyes were also hidden behind oversize glasses, her hair pushed back from her face with a tortoiseshell headband.

"Ah, excuse me," the man said. "Have we found the *Ginny?*"

In Captain Hunter's absence, Kate shaded her eyes with one hand and said, "Yes, you have."

"I'm Professor Lawrence Sheldon. And this is my daughter Margo."

"I'm Kate Winthrop," she said, beginning to feel as if she had landed on the *Minnow*. She wondered if she would get to be Ginger or Mary Ann.

"Is Captain Hunter here?" the professor asked.

"He went for some Aspirin," she said, trying not to smile. "I think he's developed a headache."

WITH THE ARRIVAL OF Kate Winthrop this morning, Cole had somehow known nothing about this trip was going to go as planned. Just to further illustrate his point, no sooner had he shown the Sheldons to their separate rooms than the younger brother of his one and only crew member, Jim, appeared on the dock, waving frantically.

The boy came bounding toward him, his running

shoes squeaking against the wood. He skidded to a stop beside the *Ginny*, his chest working for air. "Hey, Mr. Hunter!"

"What's up, Jess?"

"Jim can't make the trip," the boy said, squinting against the sun in his eyes. "He's got appendicitis."

"Is he all right?" Cole asked, recalling how Jim had said he didn't feel great just before they got into Miami yesterday.

"He's gotta have surgery. He said to tell you he feels bad for standing you up."

Cole shook his head. "Tell him not to worry. Thanks for letting me know, Jess."

"Sure." The boy turned and took off again, waving as he went.

With a sigh, Cole wondered if he should just ditch the trip altogether. If things were getting off to this kind of start, what would the next ten days bring?

The group was a recipe for disaster.

He threw a glance back at the *Ginny,* where the passengers mingled on deck, echoes of laughter drifting his way. His gaze went around the circle, landing first on Kate Winthrop, who didn't look as though she'd done a cumulative day's worth of work in her life.

Lyle and Lily Granger were both dressed in requisite orange life jackets, the nylon black belts cinched tight around their ample waists—he was guessing now neither of them could swim—and can't-wait-to-get-started smiles.

Last, but not least, Dr. Sheldon and his daughter, Margo, both of whom had already quoted Tennyson three times at last count since their arrival. An admirable talent, granted, although he had no idea how that would help them pull their weight on his boat.

He glanced at his watch. This late in the day, his options were few. He could stay in port overnight while he found someone else to crew, or he could ask Harry to go along.

This particular option came with its own set of drawbacks. But if Sam called with news of Ginny, he needed to be able to leave the boat with someone he trusted. Despite his numerous idiosyncrasies, Harry knew his way around anything that sailed the ocean.

It looked like it was Harry or nothing.

"I DON'T NEED flowers or anything, but a pretty please wouldn't hurt." Harry sat in a chair on the deck of his boat, enjoying himself immensely.

"Do you want to come along or not?" Cole asked.

"Hold on, now," Harry said. "Don't get your panties in a bunch. Anything wrong with a guy needing to feel like he's wanted?"

"Harry, I'm not kidding—"

"You're doing the pressed lip thing again. You should watch that, you know. It could result in a permanent wrinkle—"

Cole started backing up. "You know what—"

Harry smiled. "You just take yourself way too seriously, man."

"I've got a boat full of people waiting for me to take them on a ten-day vacation. I can't do it without your help. That seems fairly serious to me."

Harry tipped his head, conceding the point. "Okay, okay," he said, raising a hand. "I'll go. So what's the plan?"

"We'll leave around five o'clock this afternoon. Can you make that?"

"Shouldn't be a problem."

"Great. Thanks, man. I appreciate it."

Harry grinned. "Hey, I kind of like the idea of you owing me one."

"Just don't get too fancy with the payback list."

"I'll keep it simple. Few bottles of Dom Pérignon. A blonde or two."

"At least you're predictable," Cole said, heading down the pier.

"Do I get to bring along a girl?" he called out.

"No!"

"How 'bout the blow-up kind?"

"As long as she doesn't bother the other passengers."

"She's the quiet type."

"I'll bet."

"You can borrow her one night if you'd like," he added, laughing outright when Cole ignored him. Harry watched for a moment until he disappeared around the end of the pier, still surprised that Cole had asked him to take Jim's place.

In another world, he was fully aware that he and Cole would never have become friends. They were opposite ends of the spectrum when it came to life philosophy. Harry believed in wringing out every last drop of pleasure, happiness or satisfaction there was to be found in a given day. Cole was too busy letting life wring him to reverse the process.

The way he saw it, Cole Hunter needed to get back to the business of living. Granted, he got dealt a crappy hand with the ex-wife, but there was nothing like bitterness to turn a man into someone he didn't recognize when he looked in the mirror.

He ought to know. He'd nearly taken that road himself. Being left at the altar by a woman who admitted she'd only agreed to marry you for your money could do that.

A fresh-faced blonde with legs that ought to be illegal appeared at the end of the pier, waving. "Hey, Harry!"

"Stella," he said, recognizing her from a club in South Beach where they'd met two nights ago. She was just his type. Pretty as a peach. And young enough not to be anxious about plotting a future for the two of them. "Come aboard."

"I was hoping I could find you," she said, walking along the dock to his boat with the willowy sway of a Ford model. "Was that your friend Cole I just passed?"

"Yeah. He didn't try to pick you up, did he?" Harry asked, smiling.

"I don't think he noticed I was female," she said, giving him a hug.

"The shame of it. Did I mention he has a few issues?"

"You mean he's not girl crazy like you?" she teased.

"Is that what you call it?"

"Your reputation precedes you."

"Cool," he said, perking up.

She shook her head. "I've been warned. And here I am, anyway."

"Here you are," he said.

She lifted a shoulder and smiled. "You did offer me a tour of your boat, didn't you?"

He struggled to place the memory, found it well-hidden in the haze left by the multiple Mojitas he'd consumed on the night they met. "'Course I did," he said.

She glanced behind him, her gaze widening, impressed. "Wow, this is like a yacht or something."

"Or something," he said.

"You live on here full-time?"

He shrugged. "I try not to get too hung up on the rich boy guilt thing."

"Such a waste of time," she said.

"I'm glad we agree."

"So, how about that tour?" she said, smiling in a way that made him wonder how he'd make it over to Cole's boat by five o'clock.

"I was raised in the South," he said. "And we don't believe in disappointing ladies."

"How convenient for me," she said.

He held out a hand to lead her aboard. "Where would you like to start?"

"I think I'll leave that up to you."

"You are accommodating, aren't you?"

"I try," she said.

Cole might be right about fruit not lasting. But Harry would argue that it sure was sweet while it did.

FROM THE DECK of the *Ginny,* Kate's cell phone blinked No Service. She decided to make a quick run for the pay phone she'd seen earlier by the marina office.

Once there, she dialed in her credit card number, then waited for voice mail to pick up. She considered the fact that Karl might be able to have someone track her through the card she'd just used, then brushed away the worry. Within a couple of hours, she'd be long gone from here.

At the first blast, she held the phone away from her ear.

"Kate, where the hell are you?"

Karl. Back earlier than she'd anticipated and not pleased. She couldn't help smiling to herself as he continued. "How dare you break into my house? I found one of your little security code notes. I want that bag back with every dollar that was in it, and I mean now!"

The receiver slammed in her ear. Over her dead body he'd be getting it back.

A second message played. Karl again. This time, a little less hostile. More like his old persuasive self. "Come on, Kate. This is ridiculous. I need that suitcase, or something very bad is going to happen. Let's meet and talk, okay?"

Right. He could sit there and wait for her to show up.

Three more messages from her ex-husband played, the next two still pleading, the final one vintage Karl. She'd never heard him so angry. Or desperate. Perfect. She liked that combination. It sounded good on him.

The last message was from Tyler. Who sounded worried. "Kate, Karl has called here four times in the last hour. He wanted to know where you were. He threatened to call the police. Maybe you could give him a ring."

The machine beeped, sounding the end of the calls. She hung up. If Karl wanted to call the police, fine. She'd be happy to hear him offer up an explanation as to where the cash hidden in his closet had come from.

She turned then and headed back to the *Ginny*. Suddenly, she couldn't wait for the boat to leave. Even if it was a faded second cousin to her original expectations, all the right ingredients were there. Sun, blue sky, nothing but open water. How bad could it be?

THE SETTING SUN trailed pink fingers of light across the water as they headed away from Miami.

Harry had arrived at the *Ginny* in the wildest Hawaiian print shirt Cole had ever seen. He was an immediate hit with the passengers, especially the Granger sisters who tittered—if that was still a word—their appreciation when he complimented their matching sundresses.

One thing was for sure. With Harry around, boredom would not be an issue.

A half hour out, Cole handed the wheel over to him, and headed to the galley with a string of red snapper he had removed from an on-deck cooler. At the bottom of the stairs, he turned the corner and narrowly avoided a head-on with Kate Winthrop.

At the sight of the fish in his hand, she let out a startled yelp and flattened herself against the wall behind her.

"Sorry," he said, unable to resist dangling the line in front of her. "Didn't mean to scare you."

She drew in a deep breath. "You didn't."

He held the fish a little higher, putting them directly in her line of vision. "Harry could use an assistant in the kitchen. You can cook, can't you?"

"Of course," she said a little too quickly.

"Good. You can start in the morning. Harry will show you where everything is." He tossed the words out like a lure on the end of a fishing pole. A challenge of sorts.

She took it, hook, line and sinker. "I'll be glad to start with those if you'd like. Snapper's one of my specialties. Those are snapper, aren't they?" she asked, giving them a sideways perusal.

"Yes, they are," he said, surprised. He glanced at her well-manicured nails. "You spend a lot of time in the kitchen, huh?"

She shoved her hands in her pockets. "Gloves. They work wonders."

"I'll certainly try to remember that," he said, backing away.

"Sure you don't want me to fry those up for you?" she asked, confident now.

"We've got it covered for tonight. I'll tell Harry to count on you in the morning."

"Great," she said and headed up the stairs.

CHAPTER FOUR

Between the wish and the thing, life lies waiting.—Proverb

WHAT WAS SHE thinking?

Standing on deck with the breeze brushing her cheeks, Kate had a sudden, ridiculous urge to laugh. Here she was with her feathers ruffled because Cole Hunter had assumed she couldn't cook. Unfortunately, he was right. And she really hoped the other people on this boat were big fans of cereal.

She found a chair, deciding to take in the sunset getting ready to drop into the ocean. A stiff breeze blew across the open water, and the boat swayed gently from left to right like a child's cradle.

Her stomach tipped slightly, but the sensation was fleeting. She was probably just tired from the trip. She'd driven straight through from Virginia to Florida with little more than stops for the ladies' room and a gallon of coffee to keep her awake.

That and the thought that Karl might be somewhere behind her kept her foot on the gas pedal.

Margo Sheldon came over and offered Kate a bottle of mineral water, her smile less than certain.

"Thought you might be thirsty," she said.

"Thanks." Kate waved a hand at the chair beside her. "Sit down, please."

Margo sat on the edge, smoothing a hand across the Bermuda shorts that had replaced the dark skirt and stockings she'd had on earlier. The tweed jacket was also gone, but she still wore the white cotton blouse buttoned all the way to her neck. She pushed her thick-lens glasses up on her nose. Two seconds later, they slid back to their original position, forcing her to look over them more than through them.

"It'll be interesting to see what comes of that," Margo said, nodding in the direction of the grill and the string of fish now waiting to be cooked.

Her voice was at odds with her looks. It had a nice husky quality to it. Kate twisted the cap off the bottle and took a sip. "Yes, it will."

Margo sent a covert glance at the two men huddled over the grill like two cowpokes over a campfire. "Interesting duo, don't you think?"

Kate rubbed her thumb across the side of her water bottle. "That word would apply, yes."

"My father arranged this trip, so I really had no idea what to expect, but—"

"It's not exactly what you thought it would be?" Kate finished for her. "Me, either."

They were silent for a minute or so, neither of them elaborating on what it was they had expected.

Margo's gaze rested on Harry's shoulders, and Kate wondered at the hint of longing on the woman's face. There was no ring on her left hand, so Kate assumed she wasn't married. She was on vacation with her father, who from all appearances, might fail to be the life of the party in most social settings. She had smooth, pretty skin, and her eyes, now and then visible above her glasses, were a soft blue. Her clothes and hairstyle made her look older than she probably was. Kate sensed a loneliness in her that made her want to reach out to her, even though she didn't know her. "Tell me about your work," she said.

Margo looked up in surprise, as if it wasn't often that anyone wanted to hear her talk about herself. But she began to speak. And Kate listened.

IT WAS AN unusual turn of events. Margo was much more accustomed to being the listener than the one listened to.

She could not recall the last time she'd felt

comfortable enough with a stranger to pass along personal information more relevant than "Yes, the bus stop is a quarter block away." She once over-heard one of her physics students say that she would have made a perfect Jane Austen character, buttoned-up as she was. She was fairly certain there was no compliment to be found in the assessment, although she didn't mind the reference. She loved *Pride and Prejudice* and would have switched places with Elizabeth Bennet in a heartbeat.

But her life was in the twenty-first century, not the nineteenth, and therein lay the difficulty. She was an odd fit.

This was something that could not be said of Kate Winthrop.

She fit. In this century. This Caribbean movie set backdrop. The cover of *InStyle* magazine would not be a stretch.

It was this that made her wonder then why they'd spent the past forty-five minutes talking as if they had a bevy of shared interests to unearth. Most amazing was the fact that she really listened. Margo was far more used to the glazed-eye response she normally got from strangers. Admittedly, the finer points of quantum physics didn't exactly make for mainstream conversation. But it was what she knew.

When she began to get a little too detailed about the specifics of what she did every day, Kate—unlike most people who simply looked at their watches, announced they had some to that point forgotten emergency and flew off to take care of it—steered her toward the personal. What was it like to be a woman in a field once monopolized by men? Did she ever want to do something different? Were there any cute guys who taught at Harvard?

This was the question that tripped her up, caused her to sputter her last sip of iced tea.

"Are you all right?" Kate asked, sitting up and patting her on the back with several resounding thwacks.

"I—yes," she said, coughing again and clearing her throat.

"Was it something I said?"

"Ah, no. It's just not a question I've been asked before."

"Why not?"

"Well," she said, stalling. "I'm not exactly an expert on the subject."

"Because?" Kate posed, raising an eyebrow as if Margo had just thrown her an impossible to process piece of information.

"That's just not my area of expertise," she

managed, wiping the spattered tea from her white shorts.

"Is there anyone who can claim to be an expert on the subject?" she asked. "Men are shape-shifters. No sooner do you think you have one variety nailed, than they morph to something different altogether."

Margo laughed, surprising herself. "I wouldn't know," she admitted. "I'm not much for dating."

"The pickings are slim in Cambridge then?"

"For someone like me, I guess so," she said, adjusting her tone toward unconcerned and falling a notch or two short.

Kate studied her for a long moment. "So tell me. Who are you, Margo Sheldon?"

She'd been asked this question before. By teachers. Career counselors. But never in this situation. Never with what would make her interesting to a man as the subtext. "I have no idea," she said in a moment of brutal honesty.

"Well," Kate said. "Doesn't this trip just seem like a perfect opportunity to find out?"

"HEY, SORRY I was late this afternoon," Harry said, pulling a spatula from beneath the grill on deck.

Cole turned on the gas, then backed up a step as it poofed to life. "Didn't have anything to do with that blonde who walked you to the boat, did it?"

"Maybe a little something," Harry said, somehow managing not to gloat.

"And what'd you promise her?"

"There's the beauty of it. I didn't promise her anything. And she was okay with that."

"You don't think she was a little young for you?"

"I didn't notice," Harry said.

"Was that a Barbie backpack she was carrying?"

Harry rolled his eyes. "She wasn't that young."

"So what do you talk about with someone her age?"

"Actually, some subjects are intergenerational."

"Even when you're two or three ahead?"

"Ah, come on now. I'm not that far a stretch."

"Let's put it this way. If you two were an Abercrombie & Fitch ad, you'd be the dad and she'd be the daughter."

"Ouch."

"Those arrows of truth have sharp points, don't they?"

"Yeah, and here's one for you," he said. "I'd rather be living out my time on this planet than enduring it."

"I guess that's where our points of view differ," Cole said, putting a fillet of fish on the grill.

Harry's gaze snagged on Kate Winthrop and Margo Sheldon where they sat talking at the far side of the deck. "I'm beginning to think you did me a favor asking me to come along on this trip," he said. "Two attractive gals. And we just happen to be two single, available males. Couldn't have set it up better myself. 'Course I'm starting to think the studious one is more your style."

From the table next to the grill, Cole picked up a knife and began to slice a loaf of bread, hitting the cutting board with even, forceful strokes. "Nix the assumptions of commingling. You're not Hugh Hefner, and they're not Playmates."

"You'd let an opportunity like this pass you by?" Harry asked, amazement widening his eyes.

"How good a swimmer are you, Harry?"

"Pretty good," he said, "but—"

"If you don't want to prove it by doing the breast stroke back to Miami, I suggest you drop the subject."

Harry opened his mouth to protest, then wisely shut it.

IT WAS ALMOST dark by the time Harry Smith called out across the deck, "This way for the feast of your lives!"

The long, family-style table had been set up complete with a checkered cloth, real dishes and silverware. The two men had prepared quite a spread of food, platters of red snapper flanked by colorful grilled vegetables and several baskets of what smelled like fresh, home-baked yeast bread.

"A feast fit for a king," Lily Granger declared.

"And a queen," Lyle amended.

"Oh, yes, of course," Lily said with a laugh. "Lyle's a women's-libber," she added in an exaggerated whisper to the rest of the group. "Militant about it, really."

Kate smiled, unable to picture either of the older ladies marching in front of the White House. They all sat down and began to eat, forks and knives clinking against white enamel plates.

From his seat at the end of the table, Cole looked at her and said, "Tomorrow, we'll get to sample some of Ms. Winthrop's cooking skills. She'll be helping Harry with breakfast."

"How wonderful," the Granger sisters said in unison, actually sounding a little jealous.

"Indeed," agreed Dr. Sheldon, pushing his black-rim glasses back up on his nose.

"I'm sure Kate's a wonderful cook," Margo said.

Kate's earlier bravado disappeared along with her appetite.

The rest of the meal passed pleasantly enough, everyone sharing a little about themselves. The Granger sisters were from New York City. Neither had ever married, and they spent most of their time traveling. They'd just returned from an African safari.

Margo and her father were a little more difficult to figure out. She still lived at home and was obviously very much under his thumb. Kate saw something of herself in the other woman and wondered if she longed to break free of her father's protectiveness.

"So tell us something about yourself, Kate," Lily Granger said. "Is that a Virginia accent I hear?"

"Yes," Kate said. "Richmond."

"Beautiful city," she said. "Lyle and I spent a summer there in our teens. Nineteen—"

"Fifty-four," Lyle finished for her. "Did you grow up there, dear?"

"Yes," she said.

"Winthrop," Lily murmured. "That name does ring a bell."

"It is familiar," Lyle agreed, one finger under her chin as if flipping through the Rolodex of her memory.

"It's gotten a bit chilly." Kate pushed her chair back and stood. "I think I'll get a sweater."

She took her time going to the cabin, rummaging through her things for the single sweater she'd brought along. She'd just as soon not talk about her family. When you were the black sheep in the flock, it could get a little uncomfortable standing in the middle of so much white.

By the time she returned to the deck, the Granger sisters had forgotten all about her. Cole was currently in the hot seat, but he was even more sketchy with the details of his life than she had been. She knew no more about him when he'd finished than she had when he started.

After the meal, everyone lingered for a cup of coffee before retiring for the evening. They stood on the deck with a light breeze at their backs. Kate said good night first and went downstairs, taking a quick shower and then slipping on her nightgown. She climbed under the covers, only to realize she'd left her book upstairs. Hoping everyone else would be asleep by now, she shrugged into her robe and climbed the steps on bare feet.

She breathed in the fresh sea air, salty and warm, the smell now familiar and appealing. She looked up at the sky, awed by the vastness of it and the fact that it made the trouble she'd left behind seem a little less significant.

The book was where she'd left it, beneath the lounge chair she'd been sitting in earlier. She picked it up, then noticed someone standing at the railing several yards away, staring out at the dark ocean.

She recognized the rigid posture and stepped

back into the shadows, not sure why she didn't want him to see her. She should go, but something made her hesitate, take the unobserved moment to study his profile. Wavy and untamed, he wore his hair a little longer than most of the men she knew. His jaw was tight. One hand went to the back of his neck as though to smooth away some knot of tension there.

The light caught his face, and in that instant, she saw something in his expression that surprised her.

Sadness.

The emotion seemed out of place for him. And for a crazy instant, she wanted to know its origin. But then she barely knew Cole Hunter.

She backed away, her gaze lingering just a moment longer, before turning and making her way back across the deck and down the stairs.

IT WAS ONLY when he was alone that Cole let himself think about Ginny. Wonder how much she had grown, whether her voice still had the same sweet lilt to it, whether she had lost all of her baby teeth.

Each of these questions cut through him like a knife, and he closed his eyes against the instant pain.

Now, at just a little after midnight, he sat up and rubbed a hand across his eyes. He'd been sitting here for a couple of hours or more. This night was no different from most when he had to force himself to go to bed. Just as he sat up, Kate Winthrop appeared at the top of the stairs. She hesitated at the sight of him, then bolted to the side of the boat where she hung over the railing and promptly threw up.

She sank down onto the floor, head in her hands.

He walked over, pretty sure she wouldn't welcome his concern. Her eyes were closed. He put a hand on her shoulder, and she jumped.

"Sorry," he said. "Seasick?"

She suppressed a moan. "Please don't overstate the obvious."

"How long have you been like this?"

"I just now woke up this way."

She barely finished the sentence before she jumped to her feet and leaned over the rail again, gagging.

He went to the galley and wet a towel, returning to offer it to her along with a small bottle of pills. "Take one of these," he said. "It won't help for a while since you're already sick, but it will eventually."

He removed the lid and shook one into his palm, then held out a glass of water for her.

Hand shaking, she took it, forcing the pill down. "Can't you just throw me overboard?" she asked.

He looked down at her for a moment, then said, "As a matter of fact, I'd be happy to."

CHAPTER FIVE

A little help is better than a lot of pity.
—Celtic Proverb

LESS THAN TWO minutes later, Kate found herself being lowered into the water on an inflatable life raft. She'd followed his directions, letting him fasten a life vest around her, then guiding her into the dingy, not caring that she wore nothing more than a thin cotton nightgown or that her skin probably had the hue of green cheese in the moonlight. She was just too sick to care.

Once the raft reached the water, he buckled his own life vest and jumped over the side, tying the dinghy to the *Ginny*, then reaching a hand toward her and saying, "Come on, I'll help you in."

"This seems kind of crazy," she said.

"It's the only thing that will help until that medicine takes effect."

Intent only on escaping the nausea threatening to

consume her once more, she shimmied over the side and into the arms of a man she'd known less than twelve hours. She forced herself not to think about what might be lurking in the inky depths below them.

The water felt cool. Too lightheaded to hold on to the raft, Kate leaned against him, her back to his chest, his right arm around her waist, his left holding on to the raft. Her nightgown floated up and made a lily pad on the water, leaving her legs bare against his.

She couldn't find the energy to protest.

"Give it a few minutes," he said. "You should start to feel better soon, Ms. Winthrop—"

"It's Kate," she corrected him, perversely annoyed that he'd continued to address her that way even though she'd never asked him to do otherwise.

"You should feel better soon, Kate," he amended, emphasis on her name.

She breathed in the cool night air, willing the nausea to recede. Eventually, it did, enough that she could open her eyes and stare up at the star-dotted sky without that same wretched feeling of sickness. "This is horrible," she said, the words weak and barely audible.

"Yeah," he said, sounding a shade more

sympathetic than he had a few moments ago. "Never had it before?"

She shook her head. A few seconds passed before she managed, "How did you know this would help?"

"On my first ocean dive, we went out right after breakfast. Everyone on board was ill, including me. The dive master made us all get in the water even though we were too sick to move. Ended up with a sea full of cornflakes, but it worked eventually."

Kate moaned, an unexpected bubble of laughter breaking free from her aching throat.

"Sorry for the visual."

"At least I'm still alive enough to laugh. A few minutes ago, I was beginning to wonder."

He chuckled beside her ear, the sound unexpected and somehow soothing. "You don't seem the type to let a little seasickness get you down."

As the dizziness lessened, and the nausea remained at bay, she became aware of the arm around her waist, the chest to her back, the strong legs against hers beneath the water.

Suddenly, she had the wherewithal to feel some embarrassment for her predicament. The situation felt intimate. As intimate as two people could be when one of them had just spent the last hour heaving her insides out.

Reaching for the raft, she slipped free of his arm and turned to face him. "I feel a little better now, Captain—"

"Cole," he said.

"Captain Cole," she corrected with a half smile.

He smiled then, too, a real smile. It beamed a shaft of awareness straight through her. Along with it came the knowledge that a sheet of paper wouldn't fit between them in their current position. She kicked her feet to insert a little distance.

"Stay where you are," he said. "I don't want you fainting on me."

Imagining herself unconscious in the ink-black ocean, she did as he said, despite her overly sensitized body. "Thank you. For helping me."

"You're welcome."

The night hung dark and endless around them. They floated in silence for a long time while she battled with the desire to extricate herself from this awkward situation and the realization that getting back on the boat probably meant getting sick again. She chose what seemed the lesser of two evils and stayed where she was.

"So how do you know Tyler?" he asked, breaking the silence.

"He's my lawyer. And friend."

Cole didn't say anything for a few moments.

She sensed the unspoken question and said, "I'm also good friends with Peg. His wife."

"Ah. So what made him think you wanted a vacation like this?"

She started to say she *hadn't* wanted a vacation like this, but found herself being honest with him. "I actually talked him into selling me their tickets. I'm kind of at a crossroads. Some time away seemed like a good thing."

"And is it?"

"I'll file that under 'remains to be seen'," she said, a little surprised by the question. "I've taken up enough of your night. You don't have to stay out here with me. If you want to get back on—"

"And leave you to the sharks?" he said.

She jerked her head up. "Sharks?"

"Just kidding," he said. "It's rare to see one in this area."

She breathed a sigh of relief.

"And besides," he added, "maybe we didn't exactly get off on the right foot earlier, but do you really think I'd leave you out here by yourself?"

"I guess not," she said.

"I'd be liable if anything happened to you."

"Of course," she said, feeling suddenly deflated by the obvious explanation.

A LITTLE OVER an hour later, Cole helped Kate back onto the boat, wondering what had possessed him to put himself in this position. She'd been sick, and his only thought had been to help her. He'd then spent a half hour in the ocean with his arm around her waist, calling himself a select range of names for getting involved. He'd never known anyone to die of seasickness, and besides if Harry had woken up and found him in the water with her, he'd never hear the end of it.

He cut the thought off there, leaving the raft in the water for now and telling himself the sooner he got her back to her cabin the better.

She unbuckled the vest and shrugged out of it. The white cotton gown was now plastered to her skin, the fabric clearly outlining the shape of her body.

He quickly averted his gaze, the night air noticeably warmer on his face.

She dropped the vest to the deck and looked up at him, folding her arms across her chest as if just realizing how revealing the gown was. "Thanks for your help," she said. "I'll be all right now."

She headed across the deck and disappeared beneath the stairs. He gathered up the life jackets and put them away. That woman should come with her own set of warning labels. He'd only known her a matter of hours, and yet something told him she was trouble.

He didn't know how he knew.

He just did.

KATE SLEPT THROUGH most of the next day, waking up around midmorning to realize she had missed her kitchen duty call. She managed to quell her disappointment and went back to sleep.

At some point during the afternoon, a knock sounded at her door, and Harry stepped inside with a tray.

"Hey," he said, smiling. "Cole asked me to bring you this. Potato soup and crackers."

She lifted up on one elbow, still not sure she could force anything down. Her stomach was so sore it hurt to move.

"I know it probably doesn't sound too good," he said, "but you really should eat it."

"Thanks," she said. "Could you just put it on the nightstand? I'll give it a try."

He set the tray next to the bed. "Cole said you had a rough time of it."

"It was pretty awful," she admitted, dropping back onto the pillow, surprised by her own weakness. "I'm sure I left him with a lasting impression."

"Happens to the best of us," Harry said. "So he threw you overboard, huh?"

"Something like that." She managed a half smile. "Sorry I missed out on the breakfast thing this morning."

"No problem," he said. "Margo volunteered. She's pretty handy with a skillet for someone so…academic."

"Is that how you see her?"

"It's kinda hard to miss."

"I think there's a lot more there."

"Maybe. But women like that make me nervous."

"What kind is that?" she asked.

"The kind who makes you feel like you need to check every other word in the dictionary before you say it."

"You think she's an intellectual snob?"

"Let's just say when it comes to words, she uses a lot of the high-dollar kind. I'm of the fifty-cent persuasion."

"Book by the cover," she said.

"Don't you find it's usually an accurate reflection of what's on the inside?"

"Not necessarily."

"We'll see," he said. "You get some sleep, and be sure to eat that soup."

Once Harry left, Kate forced a few spoonfuls down, but gave up when her stomach balked yet again. She curled up under the covers and closed her eyes, wondering why Cole had sent Harry with the soup instead of bringing it himself.

AFTER DINNER, COLE went down to check on Kate. He'd found reasons throughout the day to send the others, first Harry, then each of the Granger sisters, then Margo Sheldon. But now that everyone else had gone to bed, he decided to go himself. Not wanting to wake her, he cracked the door and peered in, letting his eyes adjust to the dimness.

She was asleep, her hair spread out on the white pillowcase, the cup of soup barely touched on the nightstand beside her. The moonlight brushed her face. Her lips were slightly parted, her breathing steady and even. The sheet had slipped down to reveal the top of yet another cotton nightgown, this one pink and sleeveless. Somehow, he'd pictured her in silk.

There was a blanket in here somewhere. He turned abruptly and opened the small closet door behind him. He rummaged through a stack of clothes, lifting the suitcase at the bottom and looking under it. No blanket.

"What are you doing!"

The shriek brought his head up with a bang

against the closet shelf. He muttered a choice word or two, swung around to find Kate sitting straight up in bed, glaring at him.

"What are you doing?" she repeated in a panicked voice.

"Looking for a blanket," he said, rubbing his head. "I thought you might be cold."

"I'm fine," she said, tilting her head to look past him into the closet. "I don't need one. Really."

He closed the door, trying not to notice that the sheet had fallen down around her waist, her nightgown more than a little transparent.

She shifted on the bed, looking embarrassed now. "I—I'm sorry about your head."

He ignored the apology and said, "How are you feeling?"

"Better. Much. Thank you."

He picked up the bowl of soup and added, "You really should eat something."

"Tomorrow."

"All right then," he said, glancing at the closet again before backing toward the door. "See you in the morning."

THE SECOND COLE'S footsteps hit the stairs, Kate flopped back against her pillow, letting out the chest full of air she'd been holding.

Way to go.

Nothing like a bloodcurdling scream to waylay suspicion. No telling what he thought she had in there now. Drugs. Stolen jewelry. A bag full of cash.

Right. He was no doubt making a list of the possibilities at this very moment.

Being married to Karl had made her paranoid.

She got out of bed and opened the closet, feeling beneath the clothes stacked on top of the leather case. Still there. Thank goodness.

Maybe she'd be better off emptying the contents and hiding it elsewhere.

The mattress. She could put it under the mattress.

She pulled out the suitcase, opened it and stared down at the neatly stacked rows of cash. A little over one million dollars. More money than most people ever saw in a lifetime. By rights, it was hers. Karl had stolen every cent of it from her. Left her virtually penniless. Admittedly, he could never have managed it without her willing gullibility.

To her credit, though, she'd been vulnerable after her father died. Guilt did that. Karl simply slid into the empty spot in her life and made her believe he was the one, that here was a place to go from what felt like nowhere.

So this money had significant meaning for her. It meant she had beaten him at his own game. Greater on the scale of satisfaction—higher even than getting at least some of her inheritance back—was the fact that she had one-upped her ex-husband. In the end, she'd won.

She should be drinking champagne. Celebrating.

She went to the sink and stared at herself in the small, semicloudy mirror. But what was there to celebrate really? She'd regained a few tattered strands of her decimated pride. So what? It didn't change the fact that she was thirty-three years old, had never worked a day in her far-too-cushioned life and had no idea where to go from here.

THE WOMAN WAS a basket case.

Clearly.

There was no other explanation for it, Cole told himself as he climbed into bed a few minutes later.

Why else would she have acted like he was set on robbing her blind?

Unless she had something to hide.

He threw his feet over the side of the bed, elbows on his knees. He didn't need something like this to worry about right now. With the possibility that Sam might actually have a real lead on finding Ginny, he didn't want anything to interfere with his leaving when that call came. Like having his boat get pulled over and something illegal found on board.

Something to hide. That was exactly how Kate Winthrop had been acting since the minute she'd boarded. He recalled the way she held on to that suitcase yesterday, how she'd gotten all prickly when he'd offered to carry it to her room. And then just now, how she'd practically had a heart attack not because he was in her room, but because he'd opened her closet door.

He jumped up then, yanked on a pair of shorts, not bothering with a shirt. If that woman had brought drugs on his boat, he'd personally toss her and her fancy suitcase overboard.

Her door still wasn't locked, so he didn't bother with a knock, either. He stopped at the side of her bed, his voice clipped and angry when he said, "What's in the suitcase?"

She scrambled up against her pillow, her face nearly as white as the case covering it. "What right do you have to barge in and out of here whenever you want?"

"You're hiding something."

"You're crazy!"

"I don't think so. I don't know what you've got in there, but it better not be something illegal." He went to the closet, pulled the door open and yanked the leather satchel out.

She stayed where she was, arms folded across her chest. "Go ahead. Open it."

"Thank you, I will." He reached inside, felt around. Pulled out a handful of the sexiest underwear he'd ever laid eyes on. He dropped them as if they were on fire.

She smiled. "Satisfied?"

He stared at her for a moment, grudgingly aware that he should apologize. He couldn't find it within himself to do so.

Without another word, he put the suitcase back in the closet, then wheeled around and left.

IT WAS AFTER midnight when Harry gave up on the effort of trying to sleep.

A night owl, he had sufficiently adjusted his body clock so that rising before 11:00 a.m. felt like getting up at sunrise. He headed for the galley, grabbed a bottle of tequila and its accompanying shot glass from the cabinet where he'd discovered Cole's stash, then groped around in the half dark for a knife and a lime.

At the top of the stairs, he took one of the chairs, sat for a moment with the unopened bottle on his lap. The night was warm, the sea air salty on his lips. He dropped his head back, stared up at the canvas of sky above, white stars on black velvet.

Harry wasn't very good at being by himself. He tried to avoid the possibility as much as he could, keeping his own boat full of guests, most of whom he barely knew. He readily admitted to selfishness over any unjust accusations of generosity. The truth was when other voices were added to the mix, he could easily drown out the one nagging low inside him.

At one point in his life, he'd thought he was going to have the normal get-married-have-kids kind of existence. When that vision exploded in front of his face one June afternoon in a church filled with four hundred guests, he somehow managed to convince himself he'd never wanted that life, anyway.

"You know what they say about drinking alone."

The voice caught him by surprise, although he already recognized Margo's dry lilt. "I hadn't gotten around to that part yet, but now that you're here, I'm saved. Have a seat. I'll pour you a shot."

She took a step back. "I don't drink."

"Not even a little bitty shot?"

"I have a feeling that little bitty shot would pack a considerable punch."

He shrugged. "Can't deny that."

She looked at him for several moments, making him feel as if he had been whisked under her microscope and found to be a species of unknown origin. "I can sit for a bit though," she finally said.

He stood, pulled a nearby chair closer, even though he now thought it would have been a far better idea to let her be on her way. "Have a seat," he said.

She sat, unsure, as though he might have wired the chair with some kind of device that could go off at any moment.

"I don't bite, you know," he said, just the slightest bit irritated by her holier-than-thou manner.

She stared at him solemnly. "That remains to be seen," she said.

Amusement tinted her voice. Subtle as it was, it surprised him. He broke open the tequila bottle, poured himself a shot, downed it and then followed up with a wedge of lime. He made a face, then swallowed hard.

"Aren't you supposed to have salt with that?" she asked.

"That's the preferred method," he said. "I'm doing the abbreviated version."

"The salt and lime not really being the part that's interesting to you."

"You could put it that way," he said, again

surprised by her humor. His first impression of her had offered no clues to this part of her personality. He had to admit, it made him curious about the rest of her.

"So tell me about yourself, Margo Sheldon."

"You're the second person on this boat to ask me that. But I doubt you'd find the story very interesting," she said, staring out into the darkness beyond the boat.

"Shouldn't I be the judge of that?"

"I'd rather hear yours first."

"Mine," he said, leaning his head against the back of his chair and propping the tequila bottle against the inside of his knee. "There's not a lot to tell."

"Let's hear it, anyway," she said.

She studied him with the intensity of someone who really did want to hear what he had to say. He thought about his afternoon with Stella and realized it hadn't mattered to him whether her interest extended beyond the superficial or not. It was a little startling to think he might actually care what Margo Sheldon thought of him. But then it was probably that aura of intelligence she wore like a suit of armor. That in itself could intimidate a man into parading out every A he ever got in school just so she wouldn't think him a complete idiot. He resisted the impulse and started with the basics. "So let's see. I grew up in Savannah, Georgia. Although people usually peg me north of New York City with this accent."

She smiled, rolled her eyes. "Right. I was guessing Alabama."

"Now, now. I went to school in New York. The first few weeks there, I might as well have been speaking Swahili. People actually watched my mouth form the words. For those four years, I squeezed a little of the South out of my voice just so I didn't have to repeat myself three times to be understood."

She laughed. It was a nice sound. "Which school?"

"Columbia."

She raised an eyebrow, obviously surprised.

"Not what you would have guessed?"

"Well. I just wouldn't have—"

"Put me there."

"I—"

He raised a hand, waved away her explanation. "Truth be told, academics have never been my passion."

"So how did you get in a school like that?"

"I didn't say I was an idiot."

"But you don't mind if people think you are?"

"I'm sure there's a reason why I should be offended by that, but maybe it's more that I don't really care what people think."

She was quiet for a stretch, and then said, "There's something liberating in that, I suppose."

"Because you obviously do care what other people think?"

She tipped her head. "I've never felt that I could squander my gifts."

"And your gift is intelligence?"

"Everyone has a gift."

"Do you consider yours an asset or a liability?"

The question clearly surprised her. Again, she didn't answer right away. "On most days, I would say an asset."

"I believe Cole said you're a professor at Harvard?"

She nodded once, as though not wanting to make a big deal of it.

"What do you teach?"

"Physics," she said.

"Ah, the fluff stuff."

She smiled at this.

"So where's the liability?"

"People make assumptions," she said.

"Such as?"

"Brainy girls don't like to have fun."

Now it was his turn to be surprised. "And they do?"

"Sometimes."

He looked at her for a few moments. She had a nice face, good cheekbones, despite the glasses. "Far be it from me to make assumptions. So how 'bout that shot of tequila?"

She glanced at the bottle, then back at him. "Why not?"

"Indeed," he agreed and passed her the bottle.

CHAPTER SIX

It is the mark of an educated mind to be able to entertain a thought without accepting it.—Aristotle

BY THE NEXT MORNING, KATE felt much better. She woke up early, surprised to find herself feeling almost normal except for the dryness in her mouth, the emptiness in her stomach and the guilt that prevented her from sleeping most of the night.

She didn't want to lie to Cole. Nor did she want to answer all the questions he would inevitably have should he find out she had a million dollars hidden under her mattress.

Raising up on one arm, she peered at the alarm clock beside her bed. A little before six. Fully awake, she got up and headed for the shower, light-headed at first and then feeling stronger as the water beat down on her.

She got dressed and climbed the stairs where a

warm, salty morning breeze greeted her. The fresh air felt good after a day spent in her cabin. She found Cole on deck, staring out at the morning ocean, a cup of coffee in one hand, the sun a huge pink ball ascending the skyline behind him. There was no one else in sight.

"Good morning," she called out, doubtful of her reception.

He turned around, clearly surprised to see her. "What are you doing up so early?"

"I slept around the clock. That should last me a while."

He started to speak, stopped, then finally said, "Look, I'm sorry about last night, Kate. I had no right to barge into your room like that."

She started to agree with him, but her own guilt prevented it. He hadn't been so off base, after all. She *was* hiding something. Just nothing illegal. From any logical point of view, of course. "Well, you did save me from a slow death at the hands of seasickness," she said.

His smile surprised her. "Fair enough."

He held her gaze, and she remembered suddenly what it felt like to be immersed in the balmy ocean water with his arms encircling her. She glanced away, certain there was trouble down that path. "I thought I'd help Harry out in the kitchen. That is, if he—"

"I told him to sleep in this morning. But I could use the help. If you feel like being around food."

"Actually, I'm starving," she said. "Lead the way."

KATE FOLLOWED COLE around the kitchen, which, within the confined space of the galley, meant she basically stood still while he pointed out the location of any items he thought she might need.

She listened, apparently awestruck, while he explained the secret to making fresh bread every day.

"So that's it," she said. "I couldn't picture you down here kneading dough every morning."

"Bread ovens," he said. "Throw in the ingredients, turn on the machine, and in two and a half hours, you have hot yeast bread. May just be the greatest invention of the twentieth century."

"You don't seem like the know-your-way-around-the-kitchen type," she said, obviously amazed that a man like him could be enamored of such a gadget.

"Lot of hats to wear around here," he said, reaching beneath a counter to pull out a tin of flour, a pack of yeast, nonfat skim milk and water. He opened the refrigerator and held up a carton of eggs. "I add two egg whites to the mix. Recipe doesn't call for them, but they make a better bread."

"So how did a guy like you learn how to cook?" she asked, sounding intrigued.

"I like to eat?"

"Oh."

"You don't?"

"Eat?"

"Cook."

"I may have exaggerated my skills in that department."

"Really?" he asked, trying to look appropriately surprised.

"You knew, didn't you?"

"Your bravado was less than convincing," he said.

"I'll remember to practice it next time."

"At the risk of sounding like someone who's never heard of the women's movement, why don't you cook?" he asked.

She lifted a shoulder. "My father was never home much when I was growing up, and we had someone who cooked for me. My mother died when I was eight."

"I'm sorry."

"Thanks."

He aimed a glance at her left hand. "Never been married?"

"Divorced."

"He didn't like to eat?"

She smiled. "He was never home for meals either."

"Like father, like son-in-law."

"Actually, they weren't very much alike."

He felt sure there was a story there but decided to let her tell it when she was ready.

"So who taught you how to cook?" she asked.

"Mostly my mom. Growing up in Texas, food is a big part of life."

"You visit there much?"

"Not so much," he said.

She looked as if she wanted to ask why, but thought better of it.

They were quiet for a few moments, before she said, "And you haven't been able to convince a woman to sign on for this tour of duty?"

"If that's a roundabout way of asking whether I've ever been married, the answer is yes. Divorced as well. But she'd have died before setting foot on board anything this pedestrian."

She considered this and then, "Is there any such thing as an amicable divorce?"

"I think it's an oxymoron."

She smiled.

He put the bread pan into the machine, closed the lid and punched a couple of buttons. Feeling her gaze, he looked up, remembering suddenly what the pull of attraction felt like.

He saw the same awareness in her eyes, and they both glanced away at the same time.

For the next half hour, they sliced fruit, laid out the plates, made coffee, careful not to meet gazes, careful to give the other plenty of passing room so they didn't so much as brush shoulders.

And somehow, it all felt just a little too orchestrated.

KATE THOUGHT IT likely that people who lived in gray, dreary climates would be hard pressed to believe a morning like this really existed. The air had the salt of the ocean in its touch, and the sun threw warmth across the continental-style breakfast of fresh bread with butter, sliced papaya, mango and bananas.

Lyle and Lily were the first up, cheerful smiles accompanying their good mornings. Lyle reached for a plate and patted Kate's hand. "You poor dear. I do hope you're feeling better this morning."

"Yes, what a dreadful thing, that seasickness," Lily added.

"I'm fine now," she assured them. "Although I don't recommend the experience."

"How clever of Cole to think of putting you in the ocean," Lyle said.

"Yes, but wasn't it frightening?" Lily asked. "It's so dark out there at night."

"At the time, I would have tried anything," she said. From across the table, she felt Cole's gaze and remembered too clearly being cradled against his chest with the ocean water lapping around them.

After breakfast, they headed out across open water. The morning had been an accurate prelude to what the day would bring, blue sky, the temperature in the mid-eighties. Kate sat on deck with a book, covering her arms and legs with suntan lotion that smelled like coconuts. Margo pulled over a chair and sat down beside her.

"Where's your dad?" Kate asked.

"Doing some reading in his room. He doesn't like to get behind on his work."

"Ah," Kate said.

"Can you imagine what it would be like to live in a climate like this year round?" Margo said, her voice wistful.

"Too good to be true."

"And why's that, ladies?" Harry ambled over, catching the tail end of their conversation.

"Real life isn't like this," Margo said, her gaze falling just short of his.

"Well, sure it is," he said, leaning against the railing and folding his arms across his chest. "Real life is whatever we decide to make of it. No reason in the world why you can't have sunshine every day if you decide that's what you want. It's all about choices."

Margo looked out at the ocean, and again, Kate saw something in her face that spoke of resignation and regret. "Maybe some people have the luxury of flexibility in those choices," she said.

"Maybe," Harry said, meeting Margo's gaze head on. "Or it could just be that they allow themselves that flexibility and others don't."

From the end of the deck, Cole waved Harry over.

"Duty calls," he said and headed off.

Margo sat quiet for a moment, and then, "Do you believe that, Kate? That people shape their own lives? Or that their lives shape them?"

She considered the question, wondered about her own life. "I think circumstances make some people's choices harder than others. But yes, I guess I do believe that most of the time we end up in the places we find ourselves because we chose to be there. Even when it's the last thing we imagined ourselves doing."

"Is there a personal anecdote in there somewhere?"

"Marrying someone who had Danger, Rocks Ahead signs clearly posted all around him. That was a choice I made. Not to see them."

"You're divorced now?"

She nodded.

"I'm sorry."

"For the past year, I haven't been able to think of anything other than revenge. I blame myself as much as I blame him, but that doesn't make it easier to accept."

"No, I guess not." Margo sighed and dropped her head against the back of her chair, looking up at the sky. "Weeding out worthless men isn't something I have to worry about. In fact, sometimes I wish I could just make up another life."

"If you could, what would it be like?"

Margo looked down, her smile shy in the way of someone much younger. "Oh, I don't know. I wouldn't wear glasses. My hair would be blond. Men like Harry would really see me."

"And how do you know he doesn't see you now?"

She gave Kate a you're-not-serious look. "Men like Harry do a double-take at women like you, not women like me," she said.

"You're not being very fair to yourself, Margo."

"Oh, please, don't think I'm pitching for a pity party here," she said with a quick laugh. "I just know my limitations. Life feels a lot safer when you don't try to operate outside of them."

"I understand," Kate said. "My decision to do exactly that drove a wedge between my father and me that we never quite got past. He basically died thinking I wasted eight years of higher education to gallivant around Europe drawing pictures."

"You're an artist?"

She lifted a shoulder. "Was, I guess."

"Was?"

"I haven't painted in a while."

"Why?"

"When my father died three years ago, I realized what a disappointment I had been to him. I guess I thought if I gave it up and tried to do something he would approve of, maybe it wouldn't all seem so pointless."

Margo remained quiet for a moment and then said, "My whole life I've wanted to be as smart as my father. I never really dated because grades were what seemed important. Now I'm thirty-five and frumpy and wouldn't know how to attract a man if my tenure depended on it."

"Do you want to?"

"What?"

"Attract a man?"

Margo pushed her glasses up with one finger and lowered her eyes. "That would be a tall order."

Kate glanced at Harry and Cole who were now

sorting through snorkeling gear and laying it out piece by piece. Harry's laughter rang true in the warm morning air. "Why don't you just leave that up to me?" she said.

IN HER ROOM, Margo put on some more suntan lotion, then washed her hands at the small sink.

She glanced up at the mirror, staring at the reflection of a woman whose face wasn't ugly, but not beautiful, either. If she had to choose a word, pleasant would most closely describe it.

There was nothing wrong with having pleasant looks. It was something she never thought she cared about, but maybe she did. Maybe deep down, she always had.

Sitting outside with Harry last night, stars the only roof over their heads, she'd wondered what it would be like to know that he found her attractive.

Now, as she had then, she flicked the thought away, realizing how ridiculous it would be for a woman like her to interest a man like him. They could not be more polar opposites.

She'd seen the woman with Harry the afternoon they'd left Miami. She could easily have stepped off the cover of a Victoria's Secret catalog, her white shorts and white T-shirt figure-conscious in a way that only someone with a perfect body would ever dare wear. And the way she'd kissed him goodbye had made Margo look away, as if she'd just opened a bedroom door and found them oblivious to the rest of the world.

She wondered what kind of kisser Harry was.

Just the thought made her roll her eyes. It was not something she ever expected to find out first-hand.

What was wrong with her, anyway?

At home, her life was full and demanding. She arrived at her office by 7:00 a.m. and rarely left before 6:00 or 7:00 p.m. She liked it that way. She had the occasional lunch with a teacher friend and most evenings ate dinner with her father at a diner near their house. She'd thought many times of moving out and getting a place of her own, but she was there so rarely. The times she'd mentioned it to her father had so obviously distressed him that she'd always let it go.

The responsibility of her regular life left little time for this kind of ridiculous fantasizing. And regardless of what Kate said, it was ridiculous.

This did not explain in any way, then, why she dug from the bottom of her purse the pair of contact lenses she'd bought in a moment of rebellion against her glasses and had never worn. She put them in and stood blinking before the mirror for a few seconds before her image came into clear focus. It felt strange, and she considered taking them out and grabbing for the comfort of the familiar. But before she could change her mind, she put the glasses in their case and left the room.

THEY DROPPED ANCHOR at a good snorkeling spot near a small, uninhabited island. Cole spent the first hour or so with Lyle and Lily, giving them a refresher course of the basics. This proved something of a challenge since they refused to remove their life jackets. Even so, they seemed to have a good time, their enthusiasm contagious. Clearly, somewhere along the way, they'd figured out how to enjoy life, and he found something admirable in their blatant celebration of it.

When they'd had enough, Cole helped each of them back on the boat, spotting Kate on a float some twenty yards out. She'd opted not to snorkel this morning. She wore a blue one-piece bathing suit that somehow managed to engender more interest than any bikini he'd ever seen. She lay face up on the float, her left arm stretched above her head, sunglasses covering her eyes. He reluctantly took in the length of her. Her legs were surprisingly long for her height, her calves and thighs developed enough to make him think she worked out at something. Her body was tight and compact with smooth lines and subtle definition. Her arms were slender, tapering to hands that featured those perfectly manicured nails.

Harry walked up, gave him a playful sock on the shoulder. "Nice view, huh?"

Cole shrugged, reaching for nonchalance. "Nice enough."

"That a clinical assessment?"

"If that's your way of asking whether I'm interested, the answer is no."

Harry chuckled. "At least I know you're alive. I was beginning to wonder."

For once, he found it impossible to argue.

CHAPTER SEVEN

If a man insisted always on being serious, and never allowed himself a bit of fun and relaxation, he would go mad or become unstable without knowing it.—Herodotus

THE DAY WAS wonderfully long and relaxing. Kate felt her pasty white February complexion bloom beneath the warm Caribbean sun. As planned, she helped Harry with dinner. To call the experience a disaster would have been a gross understatement.

But somehow Harry made her blunders seem acceptable. When she burned the rice, he smiled and said, "That darn pot. Cole could at least spring for the nonstick variety."

When a head of lettuce slipped from her hands and landed with a plop on the floor, he shrugged. "Had too many brown spots on it anyway," he said, then cheerfully went to the refrigerator for more.

When she broke the tip off what appeared to be

a very expensive paring knife, he tossed it in the trash can. "Too sharp. Too dangerous. Good riddance."

And when Cole came downstairs to see how things were going, Harry put a hand on her shoulder and said, "Kate's been a big help."

Too embarrassed to contradict her culinary ally, she avoided Cole's gaze, gathering up a couple of bowls and heading to the upper deck where the breeze immediately took the telltale heat from her cheeks.

Despite her role in it, dinner turned out to be a hit. The menu consisted of a green salad with olive oil and balsamic vinegar as dressing. Pan-seared grouper over mashed potatoes. And an assortment of roasted fruit for dessert. Harry generously pulled Kate under the umbrella of accolades, and she decided then that there was a lot more to him than the playboy persona he seemed content to indulge. And Margo definitely had a crush on him. Kate noticed her gaze straying his way more than once throughout the meal. Her itch to matchmake developed new intensity.

After dinner, Harry invited everyone to go into Seamore, the dot of civilization that passed for a town on the small island where they'd docked for the night. A band, which Harry said played the best reggae music this side of Jamaica, was performing at the Pelican Bar and Grill. Exhausted from the snorkeling, Lyle and Lily planned to turn in early. The professor declined as well, leaving only Kate and Margo as willing participants. But Margo's father had other ideas about her going. "I think it would be best if you stayed here with me tonight, dear."

"I'd like to go," she said, sounding more firm than Kate had yet heard her with him. "Just for a little while."

"You go ahead then," he said, instantly deflated. "I'll be fine here by myself."

Margo looked at Kate, and then dropping her gaze, said, "No, that's all right. I'll stay."

Kate frowned, catching a glimpse of a previous version of herself in Margo's automatic acceptance of her father's will. The thought brought with it a rush of guilt, but at the same time reluctant acknowledgment that for much of her life, she had gone along with her own father's assumptions of who she was and who she would be. Their parting point had come about when she decided she didn't want to make the same choices for her life that he had made for his. She felt a too-familiar pang of regret for the resulting division between them.

She went to her room and changed from denim

shorts into a white linen sundress and strappy sandals. A few minutes later, she came back upstairs to find Harry trying to talk Cole into going with them to the Pelican. She pinned her gaze somewhere to the left of them, unsure what she hoped his answer would be.

"You two go ahead," he said. "I'll stay here and keep an eye on things. I'll see you in the morning."

"Stubbornest man I've ever known," Harry muttered at Cole's retreating back.

Kate brushed away her own disappointment. It made no difference to her whether Cole went or not. No doubt it would be more fun without him. Harry offered his arm, and they headed into town.

The sky hung dark overhead but for a sprinkling of stars, the night air warm and balmy. The restaurant was only a short walk from the boat. Harry found them a table, then flagged down the waitress and said, "A Bahama Mama for the lady. Make that two." He aimed a wink at her. "Guaranteed to put a few new moves in your dance step."

She smiled. Harry's good-natured humor was infectious. And she wished again that Margo had come with them.

The waitress returned moments later with their drinks. As Harry had predicted, it was strong, but smooth and good.

"They're great," she said, nodding in the direction of the band.

Harry stood, pulling her up beside him. "Let's show them a little support."

With a full dance floor, Kate held back. "I'm not a very good dancer."

"Then we'll make a great couple."

At first, she felt self-conscious and awkward. In addition to that, it was immediately apparent that Harry had lied. He was an incredible dancer.

"Okay, so you moonlight as an instructor," she said above the music.

He laughed. "Don't think about it. Just go with it. Everybody else is having too much fun to notice us."

Halfway through "Margaritaville," she decided he was right. She'd never seen a crowd enjoying themselves more. The vacationing group obviously cared about nothing more than making the most of this evening. Kate found herself humming along to the music, the rhythm hard to resist. It flowed through her, loosened her limbs and she could almost feel the hard knot of bitterness she'd been carrying around inside her these last months begin to loosen its grip.

The hair at the back of her neck grew damp. She let herself go and just had fun. Plain old, ordinary, long-thought-lost-to-her fun.

They danced for an hour or more. Harry had no

sense of self-consciousness; embarrassment apparently a foreign concept to him. He danced like a fool, one leg kicking frantically to the side while he held his nose and shimmied in an exaggerated version of the sixties swim.

Kate laughed at his antics until her sides hurt. "Is there an inhibited bone in your body?" she asked finally, catching her breath.

He grinned and shouted, "What's inhibited?"

A half hour later, she begged for a reprieve. She pulled Harry from the dance floor, trying to keep a straight face when he insisted that the grass skirt on the lady behind them had been made from the end zone of the Houston Astrodome.

They'd just sat down when Margo appeared at the table, still wearing the contacts with which she'd replaced her glasses that morning. Harry popped out of his chair as if someone had just hit a remote button, the look on his face one of pleased surprise. "Margo. You escaped the pop-police."

She shrugged, looking more than a little guilty. "He's asleep."

"Great!" Harry said, clapping his hands together. "The more the merrier. Here, sit down. What would you like to drink? Tequila?" he added with a knowing grin.

"Anything but that," she said, not quite meeting his gaze.

Kate slid her chair over and made room for her, wondering if she'd missed something in the exchange between the two of them. "Thank goodness you're here," she said, squeezing Margo's hand. "Harry's about to wear me out, and he's just getting started."

Harry ordered Margo a Bahama Mama, light on the rum. A new song began to play.

"Come on, Margo," Harry said, sliding back his chair. "Initiation time."

"Oh, no," she protested, sounding something just short of horrified. "I just came to listen."

"Now there's a challenge if I ever heard one," he said, taking her hand and pulling her up. "Let's dance."

"I really—"

"Can," he said.

Margo stood and threw a rescue-me glance Kate's way before letting Harry tug her out into the crowd.

Kate watched them for a few moments, glad for the immediate smile on Margo's face when Harry dipped and spun her.

"Hi."

She looked up to find Cole standing next to the table. "Hello," she said, unable to hide her surprise.

"I saw Margo leave the boat," he said. "I thought I'd make sure she got here all right." He stared down at her for a moment, cleared his throat and added, "If you two will make sure she gets back—"

"You're not leaving, are you?" she interrupted a little too quickly. Aware that her boldness probably had something to do with the Popeye-strong drink Harry had ordered her, she added, "I mean, why don't you sit down? The music is good." She shook her head. "You probably need to get back to the boat, though."

He hesitated. "I can stay for a little while."

His change of heart surprised her. Pleased her, too, if she were honest about it.

"Hey, Cole!"

Harry waved and flashed them both a broad grin, dipping Margo backward in an arc, her hair hanging in a curtain that nearly touched the floor.

"He's one of a kind," Kate said.

"That he is," Cole agreed with an indulgent smile that stood in direct contradiction to their frequent bouts of bickering.

She stared at him, unable to help herself. By any definition, Cole was a man to whom women were no doubt drawn, the reasons needing no explanation. Looking at him made her think of three different movie stars at once. Only Cole seemed real.

His smile made her heart beat a little too fast. Rare as it was, it transformed him, made her think there must be another side to him that he chose not to let others see very often. "So how did you and Harry meet, anyway?" she asked.

Cole shook his head. "He's just one of those people who appear one day and then seem like they've always been there."

"That's kind of hard to find."

"He's a good friend. Don't tell him I said so, though. He likes to think he's got me figured out. He'll get an instant case of overconfidence if he thinks he might be right."

Kate smiled. Their eyes met and held, and Kate felt a new awareness between them that was startling in its clarity.

The music changed then, fast to slow, but still with the beat distinctive to reggae, an impossible to resist soft, melodic harmony.

"Would you like to dance, Kate?" he asked.

It was the last thing she'd expected him to say. No, thank you, should have been her unquestionable response. But when he offered her his hand, she told herself there could be no harm in one dance.

After all, one dance couldn't change a person's life, could it?

THIS WAS A mistake.

Cole knew it as soon as he pulled Kate into his arms, as soon as they were close enough that her perfume drifted up and settled over his senses with the appeal of a good wine or a summer peach.

Common sense told him he should have left after seeing for himself that Margo was all right. But he couldn't shake the image of Kate when he'd first walked in the bar and saw her dancing with Harry. Appealing as all get-out in her bare-backed dress, face flushed, hair damp. He couldn't take his eyes off her.

Now, he held her in his arms. And everything about it felt too good. The Caribbean night lay clear and star-dotted above them in the open-roof bar. They moved in a small circle on the dance floor, close enough to raise his pulse and set his train of thought out on a track it had no business taking.

She tipped her head back, her neck long and graceful. "It's nice out here," she said. "I can see why a person… How you could get attached to a life like this."

"It didn't take me long," he said. "I can't imagine living in a city again."

"Where did you live?"

"D.C. Land of the commute."

"Is that why you left it all behind?"

"No. I never even realized it bothered me until I'd walked away from it."

"What did you do there?"

"I was a corporate attorney."

"Really?"

"Shocked?"

"A little. You've shed your skin so convincingly."

He smiled at that. "I'm sure you meant that as a compliment."

She looked up at him. "How did you end up on a boat in the Caribbean?"

"A client I'd done a lot of work for left it to me when he died. He didn't have any family and never made time to take the thing out himself. I'd had it a couple of years. Never used it. After my marriage broke up—" He stopped there, not sure where to go with this explanation. Talking about Ginny left him feeling like someone had taken a sledgehammer to his chest. And, too, maybe he wasn't ready to see judgment in Kate's eyes.

She waited, as if she knew he was having trouble finding the right words. "After my marriage broke up," he started again, "I realized I needed to make some changes to my life. I took the boat out one weekend just to get away. And I never went back."

Her eyes widened. "Wow. That must have been a hard decision."

"If I'd actually thought about it, maybe so. But luckily, I caught a glimpse of myself in the mirror one morning, thirty years down the road, and realized I was going to end up exactly like my client. A heck of a lot of things accumulated along the road to old age and not a person in sight to share it with."

"That's amazing though," she said. "To just one day decide you're going to be something different from what you've always been."

"It's not so difficult when you realize that what you've been isn't that great."

She stared at something over his left shoulder. He could almost see the wheels turning in her mind. He wondered what comparisons she was making. "But then that's the part most of us never get to," she said. "An honest look at ourselves."

Something in her voice told him she was talking about herself, and again, he wondered. But he didn't ask. Not his place.

Here, on this crowded dance floor, with the beat of the music throbbing around them, he was glad he'd come. Glad for the feel of her in his arms.

She looked up just then, and the spark of attraction between them took firmer hold, no words needed to confirm its existence.

He wanted to kiss her. *Really* wanted to kiss her. He was certain, too, that it showed on his face. And something—the slight shift of her body toward his, the way her eyes softened—told him she wanted him to.

Unable to stop himself, he reached out, rubbed his thumb across her cheek. "Kate—"

She stepped back suddenly, dropping her gaze to the floor. "You know, I'm really thirsty," she said. "I have a drink at the table. Do you want something?"

"No," he said, wondering if he'd misread the signals. He was rusty enough that it was possible. Either way, he couldn't deny that she was right to put on the brakes. "I'd better head back, anyway," he said. "Make sure everything's all right with the boat."

She met his gaze then, nodding once. "Okay. See you later."

"Tell Harry to behave," he said and left in spite of the fact that he very much wanted to stay.

KATE WATCHED HIM go with an undeniable sense of regret for her own cold feet.

A dance was a dance. And maybe she'd just been too long without attention from the opposite sex. The last two years of her marriage had been a joke.

And there had been no one since the divorce. She didn't trust herself to look at a man, much less date one. Her track record spoke for itself. So. That would explain her overcharged response to Cole's arm around her waist, his hand clasped with hers.

She was human. A normal woman with normal needs. And very bad judgment. Very bad. That admitted, maybe Cole had done her a favor in leaving. Given her a chance to let common sense override that physical zing.

But then common sense came complete with its own convincing arguments. Her life was a wreck. She'd allowed herself to be hoodwinked by a man presenting himself as something completely different from what he'd turned out to be. Allowed that man to squander the inheritance her father had spent his life working for. She'd made her share of mistakes. She didn't need to continue the trend with a vacation fling.

If she'd learned anything from her disastrous marriage, it was that choices matter. Choices paved the way to an eventual destination. Keeping her distance from Cole Hunter was the right choice.

THIS, HARRY DID not expect.

An hour and a half after she'd arrived, he and Margo were still dancing.

"So where'd you learn to dance?" he asked when the music slowed down again, and they'd had a moment to catch their breaths.

She looked up at him, then glanced away. "You'll laugh."

"I won't," he said, holding up two fingers. "Scout's honor."

She considered his vow, then said, "One of my students was flunking out of Italian. I minored in Italian in college and agreed to tutor him in exchange for dance lessons. He worked four summers at Arthur Murray and knew everything from the tango to salsa. There was one problem, though."

"What?" he asked, intrigued now.

"He was at least a foot shorter than I am, so something about it never felt quite right."

"What about when you tried it out with other guys?"

She hesitated, then said, "I never tried it out with anyone else until—"

"Until?"

She looked up at him. "Now."

The declaration startled him into a loss for words, making him wish suddenly that he hadn't asked that question. "Wow."

"Ridiculous, huh?"

"No, no," he said, clearing his throat. "I'm just feeling a significant amount of pressure here, following in your instructor's footsteps."

"His feet were considerably smaller than yours," she said, glancing down at his shoes.

A laugh burst free from Harry's chest, and he realized that it was his real laugh, not the one he trotted out when he was trying to prove to the rest of the world how perfectly amusing his life was. "If you get tired and need to stand on them, feel free," he said.

This time, Margo laughed. And again, he liked the sound of it. Liked, too, being the one to wrestle it free from her. He got the feeling she hadn't done a lot of laughing in her life. He wondered why and decided that at some point during this trip, he was going to find out.

For now, though, the dancing was nice.

AFTER LEAVING THE Pelican, Cole went for a walk on the beach. The air cleared his head, and by the time he drifted back to the boat, he had convinced himself that leaving that dance floor had been a wise decision.

Back at the *Ginny,* he rounded the corner that led to his cabin and came to an abrupt halt. A flash of light beamed up from the stairway. "Who's there?" he called out, adrenaline rushing through him.

The only answer was a loud thump followed by the sound of pounding feet. Cole took the stairs down at lightning speed. At the bottom, he spotted two hunched-over men scurrying like overweight mice for the stairs at the other end of the hallway.

"Hey!" he called out. "What are you doing?"

One of them looked back and then yelled at his partner, "Let's get outta here!"

Cole took off after them. They moved surprisingly fast for their size, as if they'd had a lot of practice at the art of escape. He reached the top of the stairs only to see them hop off the dock and into a small motorboat. One of them waved a gun at him.

He considered using the *Ginny*'s dinghy to go after them, but didn't relish the thought of taking a bullet just to get the opportunity to punch the daylights out of one or both of them.

"What's going on, Cole? Who were those guys?"

He turned to find Harry jogging up the pier, Kate and Margo right behind him. "I don't know. I caught them down below. I guess they were looking for something to steal." He glanced back at Kate, noticing that her face had gone suddenly pale.

"Did they get anything?" she asked, her voice neutral.

"I haven't had a chance to look."

"I'll go check in my cabin," she said quickly and disappeared downstairs.

"They didn't appear to be your typical criminal," Harry said. "Weren't they wearing suits?"

"Yeah," he said, wondering again what Kate was so protective of.

"What would they want on here?"

He shrugged. "Beats me."

"You're not running any illegal contraband between islands, are you, buddy?" Harry asked with a grin.

Cole gave him a look. "Right."

"Just checking," he said, raising a hand. "Hey, man, why'd you run off tonight?"

"I didn't run anywhere," he defended himself.

"I saw you tear out of there like the hounds of hell were at your heels," Harry said with a disbelieving snort.

"I just needed to get back. It's a good thing I did."

Harry stared at him, looking as if he suspected there was more to the story. "It's Kate. She's got you rattled, doesn't she?"

Cole ignored the accusation. "I'm going down to see if anything is missing."

"I'll look around up here," Harry said. "But you didn't answer my question."

"And I'm not going to," he said, heading

downstairs where he first stopped at Kate's cabin. He found her tucking the sheets back under the side of her bed. "Anything missing?"

She jerked up. "No. No, everything's fine."

He studied her for a moment, hit again with the feeling of suspicion. But he'd already accused her once and ended up feeling ridiculous for it. "About tonight," he said. "I'm sorry I left you there like that."

"There's no reason to be. I shouldn't have insisted that you stay. And anyway, I've never been a great dancer. My feet and my brain are on different lines of communication."

"You're a fine dancer," he said, clearing his throat. "I'd better check out the rest of the boat."

"Yeah," she said, looking as if she would like to add something else.

He waited a moment, and when she remained silent, headed for the door. "See you in the morning," he said.

"Good night," she answered.

CHAPTER EIGHT

Promise me life, and I'll confess the truth.
—William Shakespeare

SHE FOUND THE money in the same place she'd left it.

Kate ran a hand through her hair, hit with the sudden thought that maybe this was no random break-in. What if Karl had sent those two thugs to find her?

She sank down onto the bed, the possibility knocking the wind from her. She forced herself to take a few deep breaths and not let emotion get the better of her.

If they were working for Karl, they'd be back again. This, she knew. Karl was nothing if not persistent.

She told herself to calm down. Not to jump to conclusions.

It was highly unlikely that this had anything to

do with Karl. He had no idea where she was, after all. The only other person who did know was Tyler, and he wouldn't tell Karl. He was possibly less of a fan of her ex-husband than she was.

Maybe she should just ask Cole to drop her off at the next island tomorrow. She could arrange for transportation back to Miami and then fly to Richmond and do what she should have done in the first place. Handle the situation with Karl face-to-face.

But she didn't want to leave. She'd laughed more since getting on this boat than she had throughout her entire three-year marriage.

She thought about Cole and their dance.

Hmm.

Okay, so it was a nice dance.

She sat for a while, convinced herself it would be unreasonable to leave. She'd made a commitment to Margo to help her with her crush on Harry. She could hardly go back on her word, could she?

At noon the next day, Cole and Harry anchored the boat in another spot known for snorkeling.

He and Kate had managed to avoid each other throughout the morning, and he wasn't sure which of them had worked harder at it. The end result, however, had been a near comical series of sudden weaves and turns that successfully kept them from crossing paths.

Once they'd anchored, he and Harry got out the snorkeling gear. The Granger sisters were the first in line, dressed in lime green wet suits with the potential to blind if a person made the mistake of looking their way without the aid of sunglasses.

Cole handed them each a pair of orange flippers that did nothing to lower the volume of their color scheme. He glanced up to find Kate next in line, their gazes colliding head-on for the first time that morning. "What size do you need?" he asked.

"Small," she said.

He pulled out a bag containing fins, mask and snorkel and handed it to her.

"Any sharks in these waters?" she asked.

"Only one," he said, directing his gaze to Harry who was now showing Margo how to clean her snorkel.

Kate smiled, and Cole looked away, feeling at an unusual loss for words. Having been an attorney in his other life, it wasn't an affliction he associated with himself. Maybe it had something to do with the pink-and-white bikini she wore this morning, or more specifically, the way she looked in it.

Dr. Sheldon appeared on deck and glanced at Margo who was laughing at something Harry had just said. The professor frowned, then headed over to Cole.

"I'd like some snorkeling gear, please," he said while somehow managing to keep a protective gaze on his daughter, as if she were sixteen and plotting to elope.

Cole asked him what size, then pulled out a bag and handed it over. "We'll be here a couple of hours," he told him. "Be sure to snorkel in pairs."

"I'll be with my daughter, of course," he said, checking the gear in his bag.

"Actually, professor," Kate said, to this point a silent observer, "I was hoping you'd take me under your wing. Margo told me you know practically every fish there is by name." Her accent had thickened, her voice suddenly sweet and cajoling.

Dr. Sheldon glanced at his daughter, now adjusting her face mask under Harry's tutelage. The professor frowned again, then looked at Kate and said, "I'll be happy to tell you what I know."

It didn't take an Ivy League degree to figure out what Kate was up to. Cole ended up with the Granger sisters. Both women appeared to have a grand time, laughing and generally making him feel as if he were the world's most amazing guide. He decided it was a talent most often found in ladies of Southern origin, this dedication to making a man feel ten feet tall. He looked up once and found Kate smiling at him from several yards away, clearly amused.

A little while later, Dr. Sheldon finally managed to escape the *Jeopardy!* workout to which Kate had subjected him and headed back to the boat. At the same time, Lyle and Lily declared the need for a re-application of sunscreen and followed him up the ladder. Kate still floated nearby. Cole did a bang-up job of ignoring her and was halfway up the ladder when she called out, "I know what you were wishing."

He actually considered pretending not to have heard her, but even for him, that would have been rude. He held on to the ladder with one hand, slicked the water from his hair and said, "What?"

"That their knack for making a man feel like a man hadn't fizzled out with the current generation of women."

He raised an eyebrow.

"Oh, don't act like you don't know what I'm talking about. You were loving every second of it. Not that I blame you. They're adorable, and they meant every word."

He dropped back into the water, sending a wave splashing over her.

"Passive-aggressive," she accused with a smile, wiping water from her eyes.

He floated faceup, closing his eyes against the bright sun. "It's a lost art, attracting bees with honey instead of vinegar," he returned.

"They certainly had you wrapped around their little fingers."

"And isn't that the ultimate goal?"

"For whom?"

"Women."

"I'm sensing a trap here."

He chuckled in spite of himself. "No trap."

"I can only assume you're speaking from experience."

"Let's just say if I'm going to be manipulated, I'll take the Granger ladies' method of subtlety over the baseball bat to the back of the head approach any day."

Kate remained quiet long enough that he thought she wasn't going to answer. "Women don't have exclusive use of that approach, you know."

Her voice held something he hadn't heard before. She'd let her guard down, a vulnerability exposed that was completely at odds with the cool-as-a-cucumber Kate Winthrop he'd seen to date.

He grabbed one of the floats tied loosely at the foot of the boat's ladder, skimmed it in her direction, then grabbed one for himself.

"Thanks," she said, propping her elbows up on one side of her float and putting her snorkeling mask on top.

He did the same, and they studied one another for

a moment. He had no idea what to think of Kate Winthrop. One minute, he was suspicious of her, the next exasperated, then amused and now curious. "Why did you come on this trip by yourself?" he asked, sending a pointed look at her ringless left hand.

She shrugged, as she dipped her hand in the water. "I needed a vacation."

"Couldn't find any other options, huh?" he asked, trying not to sound skeptical.

Laughter floated up from the other side of the boat. Harry and Margo. Obviously getting on famously.

"I just went through a divorce a few months ago," Kate said in a quiet voice. "Not a pretty one."

"Is there such a thing?" he asked.

She lowered her chin onto the float, her gaze not quite meeting his. "Our marriage wasn't what I thought it was. *He* wasn't who I thought he was."

"People often aren't," he said, hearing the bitterness in his own voice.

"Is that from experience, too?"

"Unfortunately."

A couple of minutes passed, and they were silent, the water making a gentle slapping noise against the edge of the boat.

"Some people are better than others at hiding what they don't want the world to see," she said.

He felt the hot sun on his shoulders. "Yeah," he said.

"And aren't you?" she asked.

"What?"

"Hiding something?"

The words had direct aim, and he did what he did best. Removed himself from the line of fire. "I've got a few things to do before we head out. See ya back on board."

He climbed the ladder without glancing back, but then he didn't have to. He was sure she'd already figured out that one of his strengths was taking off when things started to get complicated.

KATE WATCHED COLE CLIMB the ladder to the boat, intrigued, and at the same time, wary. She didn't know his story, but the conclusion was pretty clear. Cole Hunter was not a man she should be having a single second thought about. She'd walked this particular plank once already. And although the recipe for disaster might have been comprised of somewhat different ingredients, it still amounted to a recipe for disaster. Enough said.

PAIRING UP WAS Harry's idea.

Margo's father had been looking forward to the two of them snorkeling together, and she felt guilty for leaving him hanging. At the same time, she felt a little rush of rebellion that wasn't entirely fair to him. As a modern woman, she was an anomaly, having made it through the entirety of her twenties with only two dates, both of whom her father had introduced her to.

Before this week, it wasn't something she sat around dwelling on. It was just her life.

But looking at Harry's bare chest and his nicely shaped shoulders, a wave of awareness for the things she had let pass her by hit her head on.

She climbed down the ladder into the water, slid her mask into place and popped the snorkel in her mouth. Without looking back, she swam away from the boat, intent only on putting some distance between Harry and herself. Maybe it hadn't been such a good idea to pair off with him after all.

For a while, she simply lost herself in the beauty of the living world beneath its roof of aqua water. The brilliant yellows and oranges, vivid purples and greens nearly took her breath away. She jumped at the tap on her shoulder, flopping faceup in a less than graceful rise to the surface.

Harry treaded water, looking at her through the lens of his mask.

"You scared me," she said.

"Where's the fire?" he asked. "You took off like somebody put jet fuel in your tank."

She struggled for a response. She could hardly tell him it had something to do with his bare chest and its effect on her pulse. "I just wanted to get started," she improvised. "I haven't snorkeled in years. It's incredible under there."

He smiled at her, a half smile that implied he was having a little trouble figuring her out, then said, "We'd better take another look then, hadn't we?"

They glided across the surface side by side for the next ten minutes or so. She almost forgot that he was there beside her until she turned her head and found him looking directly at her instead of the fish. She had the sudden sensation of falling, and wondered when she finally hit a solid surface again, if it would be soft or hard.

Ahead a school of very small, nearly transparent fish swam straight for them. Should she go to the left and let Harry go to the right? But just as she started to veer away from him, Harry reached for her hand and pulled her toward him. Together, they swam through the middle of the school which parted in a *V*.

Once the fish had passed them, she glanced at Harry, feeling the smile in her eyes. His held one as well. They swam on, and he didn't let go of her hand, tugging her along beside him, as if that was exactly where he wanted her to be.

CHAPTER NINE

To change and change for the better are two different things.—German Proverb

AFTER EVERYONE HAD finished snorkeling, Kate sat outside while the boat headed across open water. She was dying to talk to Margo, but the professor appeared unwilling to let her out of his sight now that he'd retrieved her from Harry's clutches. From across the deck, Margo gave Kate a look of resignation, and Kate wondered what had happened in her life to cement such dedication to her father.

The sun had begun to drop on the horizon when Kate headed downstairs to the galley where Harry put her on salad duty, which she handled surprisingly well. She carefully pulled apart the romaine lettuce leaves, washing them and then piling them in a large wooden bowl. Following his instruction, she threw in an assortment of toppings, artichoke hearts, black olives, crusty croutons and grated Parmesan cheese.

When the bowl was full, Harry glanced over her shoulder and said, "Hey, that looks great."

"A little better than my last kitchen experiment?"

"Maybe just a tad," he agreed with a grin.

She waited a few moments and then as casually as possible, said, "You and Margo sounded like you were having fun this afternoon."

Harry reached for a cutting board, sliced open a juicy red papaya, the knife thunking against the wood. "Yeah," he said, his voice suddenly a little more neutral. "She's a nice girl."

"She is," Kate agreed.

He cut the papaya into bite-size chunks, and then began placing them on a white oval platter. "You don't think she would get any ideas, do you?"

"Ideas?"

He lifted a shoulder. "About anything serious," he said.

"Harry, you just met."

"I know," he said, shaking his head. "It's just something about the way she looks at me."

"You mean as if she likes you?"

"Yeah, I guess."

"Anything wrong with that?"

Above them, footsteps sounded on the wood deck. Kate heard Cole's voice and then Lily's laugh.

"No," Harry said. "I just don't want any mixed

messages. Signals getting crossed or anything like that."

"Ah," Kate said. "You don't want her reading anything more into your intentions than a vacation fling. Is that it?"

"Yeah, I guess that's it," he said without looking at her.

She had to admit to a pang of disappointment for Margo. For reasons she couldn't exactly explain, she decided to save face for her. "What makes you think she's interested in anything else?"

He gave her a long look, before saying, "In my experience, there are two types of women. The ones who look at a man and see commitment. And the ones who don't."

"You think Margo falls into the former category?"

"Maybe."

"I don't think so," she said, her voice casual. "I think she's just looking to set her dad straight. And you're decent ammunition. Please don't be offended by this, but *temporary* ammunition, I might add."

He studied her for a moment, his surprise clear. "Well," he said, "that's good. Really. Ammunition. I don't have a problem with that."

"Good, then," she said. "Why mess up something that doesn't need to be anything other than two people enjoying each other's company? Something that will be easily forgotten when everyone is back home again. Nothing more than a vacation memory."

Harry smiled then, but it looked a little forced to her. She added a mental checkmark in Margo's column even as she wondered at her own audacity for interfering.

"You know," Harry said after a bit, "we could apply this same conversation to you and Cole."

She raised one eyebrow. "No," she said, picking up the salad bowl and heading for the stairs. "It's not the same thing. Not the same thing at all."

KATE WOKE UP the next morning to the sound of voices from somewhere on the boat. She listened for a moment, hearing cars in the background. They were in port. Wondering what was going on, she slipped out her door and up the stairs, running a hand over her sleep-tousled hair.

"Morning," Cole said from up top.

With a mental picture of how she must look, Kate seriously considered running back to her cabin. Instead, giving vanity the boot, she turned and raised a hand against the glare of the rising sun. "I heard some noise when I woke up. I wasn't sure—"

"Sorry," Cole said, his gaze fixed on her. "The anchor switch jammed last night. I thought I'd better get it looked at this morning."

"Where are we?"

"Tango Island. It's near the Dominican Republic."

"Oh." She felt suddenly conscious of her shortie pajamas, the thinness of the sleeveless top that said Tadpoles Are Cute But They Still Grow Up To Be Frogs. She folded her arms across her chest and started backing down the stairs. "I'll just get dressed then."

"There's some shopping on the island," he said, putting his forearms on the railing and leaning over. "There'll be time to go into town if anyone wants to."

"Great," she said.

"The shirt statement. Is that your personal philosophy?"

She felt her face growing warm. "So far."

A smile touched the corner of his mouth. "Funny," he said, "I'd have bet you still believed they could turn into princes."

"I did," she threw back. "Until I was, oh, eight or so." She noticed, not for the first time, how blue his eyes were against his sun-browned face. She took a step backwards. Her foot slipped, and she grabbed at the handrail, righting herself with something less than finesse.

"Are you all right?" he asked, starting down the stairs after her.

She held up a hand to stop him. "Yes. Really. Fine. I'd better get dressed. Shopping awaits."

"The important stuff," he said.

She threw him a cheerful wave and headed for her room, determined not to dwell on the way he'd said that or even give a second thought as to why it bothered her.

THE PROFESSOR HAD woken up with a migraine headache, so Margo agreed to go into town with Kate and the Granger sisters. While she didn't wish the professor ill, Kate was glad to see Margo smiling and clearly excited about their outing.

Cole and Harry stayed behind to take care of the boat, both advising the four of them to be careful with their purses. The women waited at the end of the pier to catch a cab into town. A brownish-orange car rattled to a stop beside them, a sign on top blinking Taxi. The car was small and appeared to be held together with several strategic rectangles of rust. Kate hoped no one decided to poke a finger through one of them.

They all climbed in the back, Kate and Margo acting as bookends to Lyle and Lily who were dressed today in green-and-white checkerboard jumpsuits, most of their powdered faces eclipsed by big black Jackie-O sunglasses. Their wide white smiles were a flashing neon banner for joy. It occurred to Kate that these two ladies really knew how to live. Lately, she'd been doing the standby version. Next flight, happiness. Forget about this one. All booked.

Lyle and Lily had obviously figured out there was only one flight.

The driver, a small man in a Nike baseball cap, sang along to the reggae tune quaking through the speakers behind their heads. He took them on a winding road that circled the perimeter of the island, the ocean just beyond the car window.

Kate had seen some beautiful places in her life. Growing up with a father on the Forbes 100 list made traveling the kind of thing that involved Blue Star Jets and islands exclusive to those who could afford a six-digit vacation.

But for sheer physical beauty, none of those places had anything on this one. The sand looked like one long strip of powdered sugar, with graceful palm trees throwing out little canopies of shade. A group of children played tag with the incoming waves, their faces breaking into smiles as the water nipped at their heels.

"It's breathtaking," Margo said.

"Indeed," Lily agreed.

"And what is it about winter that we love so much?" Lyle asked.

"Hard to remember, isn't it?" Kate said.

As they edged away from the coast, the scenic sand and sea gave way to rolling hills dotted with houses. The ones that sat high up with a view of the ocean were huge, sprawling properties, swimming pools serving as a front yard. But the farther they got from the ocean, the more noticeable the decline in size until, a mile or so inland, the houses had become small metal structures that more closely resembled tool sheds by an American comparison.

Many of them had open fronts and looked something like three-sided lean-tos. In one, she glimpsed four sleeping bags stretched out in a row, the remnants of a campfire still smoldering just outside its opening. A woman wearing a sarong-type dress lifted a kettle from the rack above it, a toddler-age boy propped on her left hip. The quick descent from multimillion dollar homes to this was dizzying. Kate considered the reality of extreme wealth and polar-opposite poverty existing in such close proximity, each having no choice but to accept the other.

"Wow," Margo said.

"Yes," Lyle murmured.

No one needed to say anything more. They were obviously all thinking the same thing. They were quiet for the rest of the drive. Ten minutes later, the driver turned onto a narrow street lined with brightly colored storefronts, the green, red and yellow doors each framed by white shutters. This area was clearly created for the tourists on the island, an oasis surrounded by a desert that was almost too painful to look at.

They paid the driver and got out of the car, the four of them standing on the corner as he pulled away in a puff of black exhaust, their previously jovial mood suffering a serious turnaround.

"Well, ladies," Lyle said. "We can stand here and feel guilty, or we can see what we might have to offer this lovely island in the way of a serious economic infusion."

"Marvelous idea," Lily chimed in. "Shall we?"

The two of them each offered Kate and Margo an arm and led them into the first shop they passed. A beautiful woman with skin the color of cocoa and glossy black hair that hung in a long braid down her back greeted them and asked if she might help them with something.

From there, the Granger sisters spotted a case of jewelry made from shells and asked the young woman if they might try on a few pieces. Kate and Margo wandered down an aisle to a table stacked high with beautiful carved wooden bowls. Kate picked one up and ran a finger along its smooth rim. "So you and Harry seemed to have fun yesterday," she said.

"Yes," Margo said, a note of wistfulness marking the word. She looked up, shook her head. "That's not going anywhere, though."

Kate thought about what Harry had said last night. "He likes you, Margo."

"But?"

"I don't think he's the kind of guy who wants to lead a girl on."

"He just wants to have fun."

"Something like that."

They followed the aisle to a display of sarong dresses. Kate began flipping through them, pulled out a royal blue one and held it up to Margo. "This would look incredible on you."

She glanced down, smoothing a tentative hand across the skirt. "It's not really me," she said. "I'd never have anywhere to wear it."

"How about here on your vacation?"

"Dad would have a cow," Margo said.

"Does he get a vote on everything you do?"

Margo looked up, flinching a little at the question. Kate instantly regretted it. "Hey, I'm sorry. That was—"

"No, no," she said, holding up a hand. "Believe me, I know how it looks. Thirtysomething spinster still living with her father."

"You're not a spinster, Margo."

"Actually, I am," she said. "Outdated as the word sounds."

"May I say something?" Kate asked.

"Sure."

Kate studied her for a moment, not wanting to overstep her bounds. Then realizing that she already had, she said, "You don't seem very happy."

"I guess I'm not," she agreed, running a hand down the length of her arm.

"Then why not change the things that are making you unhappy?"

"It's not that simple, Kate." She was quiet for a few moments and then said in a more detached voice, "I was kidnapped when I was six years old. My dad and I were at a mall. Dad was trying on some clothes, and I was playing outside the dressing room. This man asked me if I had seen his daughter, and I walked away to help him look. It was three years before someone thought they recognized me from a newspaper picture of what I might look like at that point and called the police."

"You were kidnapped?" Kate asked, unable to process the horror of what she'd just heard.

The other woman nodded.

"Oh, Margo." Kate put a hand on her arm, squeezed once, searching for something to say and coming up with nothing that remotely embraced the pain she and her father must have suffered.

"It took a very long time for me to get to the point where I could make myself not think about it, but I know my dad still thinks about it every day. And even though I'm too old for it, he worries about me."

Suddenly, Kate saw Dr. Sheldon in a completely different light. Guilt for her own unfounded assumptions settled over her. "Those years when you were gone…they must have been a living hell for him."

Margo nodded. "The part that makes it unbearable is the not knowing. I think somehow if you know for sure that someone is never coming back, you can start piecing together some kind of life. It's the waiting that—"

She didn't finish, but she didn't need to. Kate could only imagine what it must be like for a parent to lose a child in that way. It wasn't the first time she had been guilty of judging someone without knowing anything other than what she assumed to be truth. "He's never gotten over it, then?"

Margo shook her head. "He began suffering

from depression during the time I was gone. It's never really let go of him."

Kate sensed there was more, asking on instinct, "You don't blame yourself for what happened, do you?"

"Logically, no," she said. "But maybe there's a part of me that does. I knew I wasn't supposed to talk to strangers—"

"You were six, Margo."

She nodded. "I know. It's just that I clearly remember all the talks my dad gave me. Somehow, I imagined a bad man would look like one. The man who took me looked like someone's favorite uncle."

"Maybe that's one of the hardest things to teach children. That sometimes evil looks like good."

"Yes," she said, turning back to the clothes rack. She began flipping through the dresses again, more, Kate suspected, to avoid looking at her than from a change of heart over buying one. "It's not that simple."

They browsed a while longer, silent, and then Kate said, "I know what it's like to feel responsible for someone else's happiness."

Margo looked back at Kate then, her expression soft, questioning.

"My situation was very different, but I spent a good part of my life trying to be what my dad wanted me to be. Somewhere along the way, I figured out the load was more than I could carry. I was never going to meet his expectations. So I quit trying. And maybe ended up disappointing us both."

"How so?" Margo asked.

"By basically doing exactly nothing with my life."

"That's a little harsh, I'm sure," she said.

"No. It's accurate. Unfortunately. I pretty much wasted the better part of a decade traipsing through Europe trying to convince myself I had what it takes to be an artist. Now, I look back and it's hard for me to remember why I felt such rebellion for my father's ways. It just seemed so important that I prove to the both of us that I didn't need him."

Margo's eyes reflected quiet sympathy. Kate hadn't known her long enough to be certain of anything. And yet, she felt a current of understanding between them that could only come from having known a similar pain. The pain, she thought, of having disappointed a loved one. And the intolerable burden of knowing they would never be able to make up for it. No matter how hard they tried.

CHAPTER TEN

There are two sides to every question.
—Protagoras

FROM THE LEDGE of a rock wall at one end of the shopping district, Cole sat, restless. He pulled out his cell phone, checking the voice mail to make sure he hadn't missed a message. He tried to keep himself from checking it a hundred times a day, but Sam's cautious optimism fueled his hope. It was almost easier for him to accept that he might never see his daughter again than to hang suspended in possibility.

If he had to spend the rest of his life looking for Ginny, he would never give up. He was guilty of not realizing what he had until it was gone, and he prayed for the chance to make up for it.

He spotted Kate and the others coming out of a store on the opposite side of the street. Harry had gone inside the market at the corner to get them each a bottle of water. Cole started to call out to the foursome, but then noticed Kate watching a young woman who was holding a small baby. The woman was thin, too thin, her arms bony, her cheeks sunken as if she'd been giving what sustenance she had to her child. She stood behind a small display table of necklaces and bracelets made of colorful wooden beads.

Kate walked over, smiled at the woman and picked up one of the necklaces. She said something, and the woman smiled.

The baby started to cry, and the woman rubbed a hand across her forehead. Even from where he sat, Cole could see the baby's mouth move in a sucking motion of hunger. He wondered if the mother had anything to feed her.

He glanced at Kate, saw the look of concern on her face and realized she was wondering the same thing.

Kate turned and said something to Margo and the Granger sisters who were standing just behind her. They stepped forward and began to look at the jewelry, trying on first one strand of beads and then another. Within a couple of minutes, they had each decided on their own collection, and when they were done paying, the woman's tabletop held not a single item left for sale.

She handed each of the women a small plastic bag containing their purchase, her smile grateful.

Harry arrived back with the water, handing Cole one. "Hey, there they are," he said, pointing across the street.

"Yeah," Cole said, twisting the top off the bottle and taking a long drink.

"Looks like they've bought the place out," Harry said.

Kate looked across the street just then, spotted them watching her and then lifted her hand in a tentative wave. Cole held her gaze for a moment. And in a way, it felt like he was seeing her for the very first time.

COLE AND HARRY crossed the street where the four women stood waiting for them.

"Did you find all the shopping you'd hoped for?" Harry asked.

"We've made a good start," Kate said, holding up a quartet of bags.

"Excellent," Harry said. "Turns out we're going to have a little more time here than we thought."

"Is something wrong, Captain?" Lyle asked, looking at Cole.

"We're going to have to spend the night here," he said. "The part they need for the anchor has to come from another island. It may get here this afternoon, but chances are, it won't. I think it's best to plan on staying. We could spend the night on the boat, or there's a nice hotel by the beach."

"The hotel sounds wonderful," Lily said, turning with enthusiasm to Kate and Margo. "What do you think, ladies?"

"My sea legs could use some relief," Margo said.

"Actually, I think mine could, too," Kate agreed.

"The hotel it is," Cole said.

The woman with the baby walked out of the market across the street. She sat down on the wall where Cole had been sitting a few minutes before, pulling a plastic bottle of milk from her bag, then uncapping it and lifting it to the child's mouth. The baby drank with an eagerness that attested to her hunger.

Cole glanced at Kate and found her watching the scene as well. She glanced at him then, her eyes liquid with compassion. He nodded once. She looked away, then back at him, a soft, pleased smile lifting the corners of her mouth. He realized that his recognition of her kindness meant something to her. And he was suddenly, undeniably aware that this, in turn, meant something to him.

THE SIX OF them ate lunch in town at a speck of a place on the far corner of the main street. Size had little to do with quality in this instance, the food being the kind to long for on a day when there was nothing in the refrigerator but past-date milk and wilted lettuce. The menu was family style, and they sat at a large round table on a covered terrace, passing bowls of spicy shrimp and rice and washing it down with oversize glasses of iced tea.

Harry told stories about his family, each saga worthy of its own soap opera. Their laughter rang out against the heat of the day, the sound of relaxation and enjoyment. Kate thought it amazing that only a few days ago, she'd known none of these people, and, already, she had begun to care about them.

She sat next to Dr. Sheldon, who had met them in town, making an effort to look beneath the exterior he showed the world, seeing now the not-quite-truthful sheen of his facade.

Across the table, she felt Cole's gaze often enough that a low swirl of happiness began to stir inside her. She thought of the way he'd looked at her earlier, admiration warming his blue eyes. It was something she'd felt only rarely in her life, something she'd yearned to see in her father's eyes. Once she'd realized that was never going to happen, she'd set out to prove him right, and basically lived her life for herself.

She closed her eyes for a moment against this image, wishing she could erase it, and yet knowing she could not. She realized, too, that if Cole could see the real Kate, the admiration in his eyes would disappear in a single blink.

AFTER LUNCH, they took a cab back to the boat for their things. Cole had made a reservation for everyone at the Ocean Breeze Beach Resort, a charming place with rooms done in earthy taupes and golds. Kate's room had a ceiling fan that rotated in a lazy whir. A screened-in porch opened off the sitting area with cushioned chairs strewn about.

She'd just finished putting away her things when a knock sounded at the door. She opened it to find Cole standing outside, hands shoved in the pockets of khaki shorts.

"Hi," he said.

"Hi."

He hesitated, looked away, then brought his gaze back to hers and said, "The hotel offers horseback riding. The others wanted to go. Are you game?"

"Ah, sure. I haven't been on a horse in years, but I'll give it a try."

"Okay," he said with what almost sounded like relief in his voice, as if he'd been sure she'd say no. She had the feeling there was something else he wanted to say, but he backed away, raising a hand.

"Great. I'll see you downstairs then. Fifteen minutes."

THE CONDITIONS WEREN'T exactly ideal for riding, the late afternoon heat causing Kate's white blouse to stick to her back. The horses didn't seem to mind, though, flicking their tails at the pesky flies with an air of resignation.

From her spot at the end of the lineup, Kate had to smile. They were a strange group. Lyle and Lily beaming atop their squeaking Western saddles. Dr. Sheldon wiping sweat from beneath the thick black rim of his glasses. Margo looking quite elegant riding alongside Harry, who was, of course, regaling her with one of his tales.

And then there was Cole. Noticeably sterner than everyone else. Blatantly ignoring her again. Two steps forward. Three steps back.

Which she now felt somehow unwilling to settle for.

She reached inside the pocket of her jeans, pulling out the water gun she'd bought at the hotel gift shop just before they'd left, thinking it would be a great way to keep cool. Until this moment, it hadn't occurred to her to use it for anything else.

Holding the reins in her left hand, she lifted the

gun, taking aim at the center of Cole's back. The water zinged out in a straight line, making a wet circle on his shirt.

Cole turned and threw her a disbelieving look. "What was that?"

She tucked the gun behind the saddle horn, schooling her features into what she hoped looked like innocence. "What?"

He shook his head, glanced at the others who looked similarly innocent, then said, "Nothing."

Still too serious, though. Kate waited a few seconds, lifted the gun and fired again. Swoosh. The water hit the back of his head. Not bad for rookie aim.

But this time, he whirled around before she managed to get the gun out of sight. A reluctant smile broke free of his lips. "Is that what I think it is?"

"You looked a little hot up there," she said with an attempt at reason.

He smiled then, the kind of smile that reached his eyes, put crinkles at their corners. The kind of smile that made her heart do a little spin. "You know what they say about paybacks," he said.

Unfortunately, she did.

AFTER THE RIDE, they all changed into swimsuits and went down to the pool. Everyone except Cole.

Kate and Margo sat under an umbrella sipping at fruit drinks the waitress brought them in coconut shells that served as cups. They talked about Margo's love of teaching, and Kate envied her passion and dedication. It made her even more aware of the current aimlessness in her own life.

Margo spotted Harry across the pool, and suddenly she became absorbed in the book on her lap. Kate pulled one from her own beach bag, trying to get interested in it, but finding herself mostly just watching for Cole.

When he didn't show up after an hour or so, she told herself he'd been bluffing about the payback. She'd kind of expected a dunk in the pool or maybe a glass of water over the head. But then he didn't really seem like the type for pranks or silliness.

"I wonder what that is," Margo said.

Kate lowered her sunglasses and took a look. Two young boys were setting up a microphone and a platform on the other side of the pool. They ran cords to a pair of speakers and soon upbeat music began to throb from them.

"Looks like they're having some kind of entertainment," Kate said.

A couple of minutes later, a man wearing wild swimming trunks and an orange T-shirt with Ocean Breeze Beach Resort written across the front got up on the platform and tested the mike. "Hello, everyone! I'm Randy Hartman, formerly from Michigan where winter and I did *not* get along. I finally left her for this beautiful place you made such a wise choice in picking for your vacation. Welcome to paradise! Am I right? Is this paradise?"

Someone let out a wolf whistle, and the crowd began to clap and cheer.

"All right, then," he said, throwing a fist in the air. "Let's get started with some fun. Good-looking group of folks out here today. Especially, you ladies! I can tell this is going to be a great contest."

The microphone made a squawking noise, and he adjusted it before saying, "We're going to start out this afternoon with a little Tango Island Idol."

Taking the cordless microphone with him, he walked around the pool, eyeing people as he walked by. He stopped beside Kate's chair, looked down at her and smiled. "Our first contestant this afternoon is Ms. Kate Winthrop. I understand she'll be singing a song of her choice for us." He reached for her hand, tugging her up from her seat.

"What?" she said, hanging back.

"Come on, now," he said, smiling. "No changing your mind. Thanks for being the first to sign up, Kate. It's always good to have a brave soul out in the audience. Come on over. You'll start today's lineup."

"Wait," she said, holding up one hand. "I didn't sign up—"

"Now, now, don't go shy on me," he said. "You're going to give the rest of these ladies the courage to enter."

Margo began to clap. "Let's hear it, Kate!"

She sent a glance around the pool, spotting Cole where he now stood with Harry at the bar.

Cole smiled at her, then raised his glass in salute and mouthed the word, *Touché*.

THAT NIGHT, THE whole group met for dinner at a restaurant just down from the hotel.

Lyle and Lily insisted that they all wear their new dresses, and as they headed down the beach to meet the men who had gone on ahead, Kate was glad they had. She liked the casual feel of it. She carried her sandals in one hand, enjoying, too, the squish of sand between her toes. The island life had begun to grow on her.

They arrived at the restaurant just as the sun dropped in a fireball burst of color against the blue horizon. The hostess went off to check their reservation, and they stood outside in the balmy evening air, chatting like four women who had known one another for much longer than the few days they had.

"You would have won if it hadn't been for that guy from Jersey."

She turned around to find Cole looking down at her with amused eyes. Harry and Dr. Sheldon stood just behind him, both staring at Margo in her sarong dress with very different expressions on their faces. Harry's resembled something close to *wow* while the professor merely looked worried. Margo walked past them into the restaurant, and they both turned and followed her as if on cue.

"And that's supposed to make me feel better?" Kate asked, refusing to acknowledge the smile in Cole's voice. "Consider me repaid."

"Oh, I do," he said, his smile entirely too appealing. And even if she'd wanted to stay mad at him, she didn't think she could have.

COLE HAD EATEN at the Sand Dollar too many times to count. The food was known as some of the best in the Caribbean, but tonight, his mind wasn't on the food.

His thoughts were consumed by Kate.

Kate, whose laughter had become a familiar sound in the past few days. He looked forward to hearing it, found himself listening for it.

Kate, who looked like a goddess in that dress. He could barely keep his eyes off her, trying to look anywhere but in her direction.

For all the good it did.

From his chair across the table from hers, he caught the scent of her perfume as the sea breeze wafted it in his direction.

She was getting under his skin.

The question? What was he going to do about it?

COLE SPOTTED HER from the edge of the beach, just out from the hotel. It was late, but he was too restless to go to bed. He'd headed outside, thinking a walk would deplete some of the energy that felt like a rocket in his chest.

He let his heels sink into the sand and shoved his hands deep into the front pockets of his jeans, studying her profile in the night-shadowed stillness. Common sense told him he should turn and walk away. Leave her alone. Drawn to her, he couldn't find the will to turn back.

He walked across the beach, stopping just behind her. "You shouldn't be out here by yourself," he said.

She glanced up. He'd expected surprise on her

face, but it wasn't there, and he wondered if she had somehow known he would come. "The sea air felt good," she said. "I wasn't quite ready to go to bed yet."

"Me, either," he said, sitting down beside her. "The ocean is addictive, isn't it?"

"Yes," she said. "It's so peaceful. Out here, my real life seems very far away."

He didn't answer immediately, then finally admitted, "Maybe that's why it suits me so well."

"Nothing permanent? Just keep moving?"

"Something like that."

"I guess that works except for one thing."

"What's that?"

"You can't escape what's inside you."

The waves lapped at the sand in a gentle melody of whish-whish, slap-slap. They sat in silence for a while. He couldn't bring himself to acknowledge that Kate was right, even though he knew she was. He carried the loss of his daughter around inside him, guilt for his own mistakes the noose around his neck. "What you did for that woman and her baby this afternoon," he said. "It was nice. Real nice."

She stared out at the dark ocean. "Do you ever wonder why some of us get such great lives and some of us don't?"

"Sometimes."

She leaned forward, propping her arms on her

knees, not looking at him. "I look at people like her and I think how crazy it is that I've—" She broke off there, pressing her lips together.

"That you've what?" he asked.

She made a small sound that wasn't quite a laugh, more like a sob. He waited, quiet, until she said, "Oh, that I've made such a mess of what I've been given."

He heard her attempt at lightness and recognized her failure. "It couldn't be that bad," he said.

She did laugh this time, running a hand across the back of her neck. "No. It is. Trust me."

"Maybe you're being a little hard on yourself."

She shook her head. "Actually, that's the problem. I haven't been hard enough. When you don't let yourself look too closely at something, it's easy to go along buying your own B.S. And then one day, someone holds up a mirror, and you see exactly what you haven't been letting yourself see. That's what that woman was for me this morning. A mirror." She hesitated, and then said softly, "I didn't like what I saw."

Of all the conversations he might have imagined the two of them having out here, this would not have been one of them. He thought about the woman who'd arrived in Miami at the beginning of the trip, a little jarred to realize this Kate barely resembled her. "What is it you regret?" he asked.

"Most? Letting myself believe that it didn't matter what I did with my life because regardless of the choice, I was never going to live up to my father's expectations."

"What exactly did he expect?"

She didn't answer for a moment, and then said, "I think he expected me to be him. To walk the same path he walked. He grew up poor. *Really* poor. His dad was a coal miner. He died of black lung disease when my father was twelve, and he had to grow up fast. He was determined to have a different life, and he did. At twenty-four, he patented this bottle capping system that made him a multimillionaire by the time he was thirty."

"Impressive," he said.

"He was an impressive man. But he could never stop working, you know? I guess what happened early in his life shaped him so completely that he couldn't be anything other than that same driven-to-succeed boy."

"And he wanted to see the same drive in you?"

She lifted a shoulder. "I'm not really sure what he wanted. My grades were never high enough. My choice in colleges not up to par. The fact that I wanted to be an artist not worthy of a conversation."

"That's tough," he said.

"For a long time, I was just mad. And then I think I decided to prove him right. So I became the spoiled little rich girl he never wanted me to be. And basically just completely screwed up my life."

"You don't look very screwed up."

"Don't let the package fool you."

"So what kind of artist are you?"

"I used to paint."

"And you don't anymore?"

She shook her head. "Not for a long time."

"Why not?"

"I'm not sure if I was afraid I wasn't any good. Or afraid that I was."

"You know, people spend thousands of dollars in therapy trying to answer questions like that."

She smiled.

"I suspect you already know the answer though," he said.

She looked at him, and he could see the surprise in her eyes. He wondered how long it had been since she thought someone might believe in her.

The night cloaked them in darkness, the hotel lights casting shadows behind them, across their faces. It made for an incredible sense of intimacy, as though they were the only two people there.

They looked at each other for a long time. For the life of him, he couldn't look away. He reached out and touched her cheek, brushed away a single tear. Time seemed suspended in motion, the silence punctuated by the sound of their breathing. He remembered what it was to want a woman, the way need slowed the blood to a steady throb.

"Cole?" His name was part question, part plea.

He put a finger to her lips, not trusting his voice. He lowered his head, and her eyes slid closed as his mouth settled onto hers.

She kissed him back, her hands slipping up to link around his neck. He pulled her close, and there was none of the awkwardness he remembered from the other first kisses in his life. This seemed like something both of them had been expecting, something that demanded exploration.

She was soft beneath his hands, and all he could think was that he didn't want to stop kissing her, that he'd like it to go on until he could figure out why this felt so different.

HARRY WAS ALL stirred up, and he didn't even know why.

He meant what he'd said to Kate about signals getting crossed and mixed messages where Margo was concerned. Even though it made him sound like a complete jerk. Even though he probably was one.

But then what was worse? Pretending to be something other than what he was and surprising everybody with it after someone's feelings got hurt? Or just being up front about it? No harm, no foul.

To Harry, this was completely logical. It didn't explain, though, why something in his midsection dropped when he walked through the lobby of the hotel and spotted Margo outside on the veranda. She sat on one of the wicker couches with a book in her lap. Her eyes, though, were focused on something off in the distance.

He stopped for a second and looked his fill unobserved. Wow. She did look amazing tonight. It was the same Margo, just a brighter, more polished version. She wore her hair pulled back in a ponytail that hung to the middle of her back, her only jewelry a simple pair of pearl earrings.

The Granger sisters mentioned earlier that Kate had given Margo a little makeover, and the results were indeed spectacular. The bookish Harvard professor had been replaced with a knockout of a woman.

In all fairness, he should leave her alone, but he found himself walking over to stand by her chair. "Hey," he said, faltering under a moment of uncertainty.

She jumped a little, looking around and blinking once. "Hi," she said, closing the book in her lap.

"Care to have a drink or somethin'?" he asked, wondering why that suddenly sounded so lame.

She looked at him, started to shake her head, then said, "Oh, why not."

He pulled up a chair next to hers. "Under that enthusiastic response, I, of course, am buying. What's your pleasure, ma'am?"

"My pleasure," she said, the words soft and low. Something unexpected tightened in his gut, and again, he experienced an uncharacteristic moment of floundering. Knowing how to talk to women had never been one of his hang-ups. He'd figured out somewhere along his path to recovery from being dumped at the altar that not caring will do that for a person.

A waitress came outside and asked if they would like anything. Margo ordered an orange juice. He followed her lead and asked for pineapple juice.

"Good dinner tonight," he said once the waitress left.

"Yes. It was," Margo replied. "You took off kind of fast once it was over."

"Yeah," he said, not sure how to explain what he wasn't sure he understood himself.

She studied him for several seconds, then exhaled

a quick sigh, as if she resented having to say what she was about to say. "Look, Harry, I get it, okay? You're not a permanent kind of guy. I may not have been around the block too many times, but even I could see that from moment one. You don't need to worry. I have no expectations. That really isn't such a bad place to be. It makes things much simpler. So the next time you're hit with the urge to avoid me, just remember that I'm not chasing you."

He opened his mouth to respond, but closed it just as quickly because he had no idea what to say. She had so nailed him that to deny it would be an insult to her considerable intelligence. "Margo—"

The waitress was back with their drinks. She placed them on the small round table in front of them, moisture beading the sides of the tall, skinny glasses. He thanked her, and she moved to another couple who had just sat down on the other end of the veranda.

"As a matter of fact," Margo said, standing, "I think I'll head up. I'm feeling a little tired from all that sun today."

Harry did a poor job of hiding his surprise. His eyes widened and his mouth went slack.

"Good night, Harry," she said and headed down the steps onto the walkway that led to the guest rooms.

He stood, too late, resisting the urge to call her back. Once she was out of sight, he sat back down, propping his elbows on the sides of the wicker chair and making a tepee of his fingers. He forgot about their drinks until the ice in the glasses had melted and watered the juice down so he no longer had any desire for it.

CHAPTER ELEVEN

Every path has its puddle.—English Proverb

KATE GOT UP early, long before the sun reclaimed its spot in the Caribbean sky. Actually, she wasn't sure she'd ever gone to sleep. She lay in bed with her eyes closed, lingering somewhere between full consciousness and a dazed state of fatigue in which her brain refused to shut down.

And little wonder.

Kissing Cole Hunter. That, she had not anticipated. And had no idea what to do about it now.

She left the room in search of coffee, and after purchasing a cup from the breakfast bar just off the lobby, she sat in a chair by the pool, replaying the night as she had a dozen times since he'd walked her to her room and left her at the door.

A single moment stood out in her mind. Standing there in front of him, the sconce light next to the door illuminating his face clearly enough that she could see something different in his eyes. A new awareness. A new interpretation of who he thought she was.

She'd shown him a piece of herself last night that she'd never really shown another living being. Let her guard down so completely, that even now, remembering it, she felt as if she had just run out in the middle of a New York City intersection without any clothes on. Just her. Right there for everybody to see.

It was painful to think about. She was tempted to sit here all day with her eyes squeezed shut, refusing to look at any of it. And yet, deep down, there was a little spot of something that almost felt like relief.

She thought about her relationship with her father. For so long, it had been the monster in her closet. She'd piled every large boulder she could find in front of it because letting it out wasn't an option.

From this vantage point in her life, she felt ashamed of the road she'd taken. Ashamed of the fact that he had died without the two of them ever finding common ground. There was nothing but tragedy in that, in knowing she would never have another chance to make something wrong, right.

Last night, she'd let Cole see some of this. She'd opened the door, and he'd gotten a pretty clear glimpse of the interior. And here was the thing. He hadn't run screaming into the night.

She opened her eyes now, and the sky lay above her in a ribbon of shimmering blue. And that was the color that best described her today. Bright blue. Just like the sky.

COLE AND HARRY headed for the marina at just after seven to check on the boat. Cole navigated the hotel's Jeep convertible along the winding street through town and then hit the slightly wider road that ran beside the ocean.

He glanced at Harry who was resting his head against the back of the seat, dark sunglasses covering his eyes. "You're awfully quiet this morning."

"Thinking," he said.

"About?"

"What else?"

"Women."

"Women."

"Any one in particular?"

"Maybe."

"Margo?"

"I'm a jerk."

"If you're making that declaration with respect to the fairer sex, you can hardly expect me to contradict you. You like being a jerk. Isn't that what keeps you moving on to greener pastures?"

"It used to seem like a really excellent game plan."

"And it's no longer excellent?"

"I don't know."

Cole let out a low whistle, then shook his head. "I never thought I'd live to see it. The conversion of Harry Smith."

Harry gave him a look over the rim of his sunglasses.

"I wouldn't go so far as *converted*," he said.

"Slipping, maybe," Cole said.

"I could throw that one right back at you."

"That doesn't mean you'd be right."

"So how do you explain kissing Kate on the beach last night?"

Cole kept his gaze fixed on the road. "I won't even ask how you managed to witness that."

"I took a walk after dinner. Seems like I wasn't the only one with the idea."

"It was just a kiss," he said.

"A long one," Harry said.

"Did you stay and take notes?"

Harry laughed. "I was going to stay and cheer you on. I mean it's been what? Two years?"

"I haven't exactly been keeping track."

"That's my job. It's been two years."

"Thanks for the reminder."

"So did it make up for the wait?"

"Harry."

"Legitimate question."

He looked out at the ocean, unwilling to let Harry see his face when he answered. "Yeah," he said. "It made up for it."

Harry threw a fist straight up. "Well, all right! It's about time."

Cole tried not to smile. "You can officially fold up your save-Cole-Hunter-from-himself tent and find someone else to sponsor."

"Oh, but there's more fun to be had, I'm sure," Harry said, grinning.

"I don't think the fun is going to go anywhere beyond last night," he said.

Harry's smile dropped as if Cole had just made off with his favorite pair of Tommy Bahama swimming trunks. "Oh, I get it. One kiss, and you're done."

"It's not what you think, Harry."

"So what is it then?"

"*She's* not what you think," he said, remembering Kate's face in the moonlight, his own surprise at hearing her soft confession.

"What you're saying is she's not fling material."

"No," Cole said, "and in case you hadn't noticed, neither is Margo."

"Yeah," he said. "I already figured that one out."

"So what's with your long face this morning?"

"Margo said she's not chasing me."

Cole laughed. He couldn't help it.

"Oh, sure, go ahead and have a good chuckle at my expense."

"Isn't that what you want?"

"Yeah," he said. "'Course, it is."

"Well?"

"Well. Nobody wants to be thought of as a jerk."

"Coming from Savannah, I feel sure you've heard that old saying, 'You can't have your cake and eat it, too'."

"Once or twice," he said, giving him a look.

"Come on, Harry," he said, landing him a sock on the arm. "Where's your sense of humor? Wasn't this your game plan?"

"I 'spose," he conceded without grace.

"But now that you're out in the middle of the field, you think you might want to change directions."

"Heck, no," he said defensively.

"You just don't want to be a jerk?"

"Right."

"Right."

"I'm sure your motives are nothing short of selfless," he said.

"You're just full of yourself this morning, aren't you?" Harry said, failing to hide his disgust. "Amazing what a kiss will do for a man who's been without for too long."

Cole shook his head, smiling, and they drove the remaining distance to the marina in silence. He pulled into a parking space, and they got out, then walked the pier to where the *Ginny* was docked. Two men wearing tank tops and colorful shorts stood beside the boat.

"This your boat?" the taller one asked.

"Yeah," Cole answered. "Something wrong?"

"Our night watchman heard a noise and found a couple guys on board around 3:00 a.m. He said it seemed like they were looking for something, but they took off as soon as he yelled at them."

Cole glanced at Harry.

"Again?" Harry said.

"Thanks, guys," Cole said. "We'll take a look around."

Harry started at the bow of the boat. Cole started at the stern. A couple of the doors had holes in them, as if someone had rammed them with a crowbar. Harry came back to report the same of the ones he'd checked out. "This seems a little too suspect to be a coincidence," he said. "Anything missing?"

"Nothing of mine," Cole said. His mind zipped from one possibility to another, with nothing remotely plausible coming up as a likely explanation.

The guy from the pier walked on board. "Sorry

about the damage," he said, "but this kind of thing happens a lot. That's why we have the night watchman, but I guess he didn't get here in time."

"You get a lot of break-ins?" Harry asked.

"Unfortunately," he replied.

"Let's take one more look around," Cole said.

"Too bad they didn't mention that before you left your boat here overnight, huh?" Harry said in a low voice.

"Yeah," Cole replied. "I doubt it would be a big boon for business."

They checked out the engine only to discover it had apparently been treated to the same crowbar treatment.

"Looks like we'll be spending another night," Cole said.

"Looks like," Harry agreed.

KATE AND MARGO ate breakfast together. They'd just gotten the check when Harry walked through the restaurant and over to their table.

"Well, ladies," he said, planting his palms on the back of an empty chair, "it's another day of fun and sun at the Ocean Breeze Beach Resort. The *Ginny* met with another minor setback."

"What kind of setback?" Margo asked.

"A crowbar with a mission."

Kate's stomach plummeted. "What do you mean?"

"Probably just somebody looking for something valuable they can sell," Harry said.

"Hmm," she murmured. Since they'd arrived on Tango Island, she'd barely let herself think about the money she'd hidden in her hotel room. With a sick feeling, she wondered now if this incident had anything to do with the guys who'd broken onto the boat the night they'd come back from dancing.

"Where is Cole?" she asked.

"He's working on getting some repairs done."

"Is there anything we can do to help?"

"I think he's got it under control. You two up for going to the beach?"

She glanced at Margo, who was doing a poor job of looking disinterested. Kate felt a sudden need to be alone, to let the panic knotted up inside her unravel. "You guys go on. I'm going to run back to my room. I'll join you in a little while."

"Are you sure?" Margo asked.

"Positive," she said.

"Okay," Harry said, "we'll save you a chair."

They headed out of the restaurant, stopping to chat with Lyle and Lily who had just come in. She heard Harry updating them on the boat situation. She decided to go out the back way, following a winding stone walkway to her room, where she let herself inside only to slide down the closed door and put her head on her knees.

What. If.

What if?

The question rang in her ears even as she told herself to get a grip. *Could* this have something to do with Karl? If it did, she couldn't imagine that he or whoever he might have hired to find her would have managed to maintain any degree of subtlety at this point. But then she guessed a crowbar didn't exactly qualify as subtle.

Maybe she should go home.

The thought settled and took root. If there was any possibility that this had something to do with Karl, she couldn't take a chance that anyone else might get hurt. The very thought made her feel ill.

And then there was last night. Cole and last night, to be specific.

She remembered the two of them sitting side by side, shoulders touching. As hard as she'd tried not to think about him this morning, he was *all* she'd been able to think about.

It was this reality that cemented her decision. She should go home. Get her life in order. The last thing she needed to do was set herself up for a regretful parting from Cole Hunter. Better to go now before the regret part got more of a foothold than it already had.

This suddenly seemed like the only possible solution. She headed for the closet, pulled out her suitcase and started throwing clothes inside. She'd just finished packing up toiletries and makeup when someone knocked at the door.

"Just a minute," she called out and then headed across the room with her makeup bag in hand.

She opened it to find Cole standing just outside. "Hi," he said.

"Hi." Her voice sounded like a balloon from which the air had just been let out.

"You heard about the boat?"

She nodded. "I'm sorry."

"It's all fixable," he said. "Shouldn't take that long."

"Any idea what happened?" she asked.

"The marina said they've had a few break-ins recently. Somebody looking for something to sell."

"Oh," she said, glancing down at her hands as a surge of something like gratitude welled up inside her. Unlike the last time, there was nothing in his manner to indicate he thought she had anything to do with it.

"What's that?" he asked, his gaze swinging to the suitcase on her bed.

She didn't answer for a moment, not sure what to say. "I'm going to head back to Miami, Cole."

He stared at her, then shook his head. "Why?"

She shrugged and tried to smile. "I don't know. The last time this happened, you were pretty convinced I had something to do with it—"

A maid wheeled a cart by, threw them both a smile and said good morning in a singsong voice. They both answered back, subdued.

"May I come in?" Cole asked, his gaze direct.

"I should finish up," she said. "Find out what kind of transportation is available."

"Kate," he said. "Please."

"All right." She stepped back and let him in.

He crossed the room to stand by the window, looking out at the pool where two young girls took turns off the diving board. "I'm sorry," he said. "For accusing you before. I was out of line."

This was the last thing she wanted him to say. He had no idea exactly how in line he was. "You don't need to apologize," she answered.

"Yeah," he said, turning to look at her. "I do."

"Cole—"

"Let me finish," he said.

She folded her arms across her chest, sitting down on the edge of a chair and forcing herself to look at him.

"I—" he started, then stopped. "Trusting other people doesn't come easy for me these days. My wife...our divorce kind of left me in a place I never imagined being. There was a lot of bitterness between us." He stopped again, and a few moments passed before he spoke. "I have a daughter. Ginny. She was six the last time I saw her. That was two years ago."

Kate discovered that she'd been holding her breath. She released it in a little whoosh, realizing that he had named his boat after his daughter. "But why?"

"My ex-wife, Pamela, took her and disappeared one day. She left a note saying I should have appreciated them while I had them."

"Oh. Cole." She had no idea how to respond to this. There wasn't a single word that seemed remotely appropriate. "I'm so sorry."

He looked at her then. "I'll find her. I won't stop looking until I do."

She nodded, suddenly understanding so many things about him.

"I'm telling you this," he continued, "because I guess I kind of keep a wall around myself. What I've just told you isn't an excuse, but maybe—"

"Don't," she said, holding up one hand. "You don't need to."

"Yeah," he said. "I do. Last night—"

He broke off there, and she knew what he was going to say before he said it. After last night, he thought he knew her. That she wasn't the kind of person who would bring trouble along with her on this vacation. A sudden tidal wave of guilt washed over her. Whether Karl had anything to do with those break-ins or not, she was hardly the person Cole was starting to believe she was.

"I'm sorry about all that," she said. "I never meant to drag you through my personal history."

"You didn't drag me," he said. "Let me finish what I was going to say."

She pressed her lips together and waited.

"It's been a long time since I've let anybody get that close. I think maybe seeing the hard stuff in someone else's life reminded me I'm not the only one trying to get past something difficult. I made a lot of assumptions about you in the beginning, Kate. I owe you an apology for that. I'm sorry."

At this point, she would have welcomed a sudden opening in the floor. "You don't owe me anything," she said, overwhelmed with the urge to come clean, tell him why she'd come on this trip, that she had, like his wife, been on her own mission of revenge.

"Clearly," he said, "you're not who I thought you were."

He watched her with the same look in his eyes she'd glimpsed last night. Only now, it was one more reminder of her own deceit. She stood up, then started folding the clothes on her bed and dropping them into the suitcase.

"Stay, Kate," he said.

She didn't look at him. She couldn't. "I really need to get back."

"Hey."

He moved to stand beside her, reaching out and putting a hand on her arm. Something dissolved inside her, and she realized that she had completely deluded herself about what last night had meant to her. Suddenly, she was back in that exact moment where she could gladly shut out every single problem she'd ever created for herself and let herself believe there was only this.

She looked up at him, aware that all of what she felt showed in her eyes. She could not blink it away, dismiss it with some flip comment.

He traced a finger along her jaw, the tip coming to rest on her lower lip. Amazing that she'd lived this long without once feeling this way. And she could not imagine how she would ever convince herself that anything short of this would be worth having.

"Kate," he said, leaning in to kiss her. All the

hours since they'd last touched melted away, and she couldn't remember why ending it before had seemed so imperative.

She put her arms around his neck, finding that they fit just as well now as they had last night. They kissed for a long time, like two people who had just discovered the excitement of it and weren't about to let it go.

The window off Kate's bedroom had been left slightly cracked. From outside, she heard the buzz of a lawn mower, laughter from children playing in the pool. She was aware of the world beyond the two of them, and at the same time, what was happening here, between Cole and her, seemed as though it could take up as much space as they would allow it.

In the back of her mind, she realized she'd never felt this way with Karl, not even close. How sad was that? Sadder still, she thought, to know that where love was concerned, the only thing she had to show for her three plus decades of life on this planet was a boatload of regret.

She stepped out of Cole's arms then, walked to the window and pressed her fingertips to her lips, a little stunned to discover they still throbbed with the feel of him.

"Kate," he said. "You can't leave now."

She wanted to ask him what now meant. *Now*

that they'd shown each other their weaknesses, or at least a portion of them? Or *now* that they'd discovered this connection with one another? But then it didn't really matter which now. It was clearer to her than ever that leaving was the wisest choice. "I'm glad I came," she said, staring out the window so that she didn't have to look at him. "But this—" She waved her hand in a circle meant to encompass the two of them and what had just happened. "We both know this would be a mistake."

"Would it?" he asked softly.

"Oh, yes," she answered in an equally soft voice. "It definitely would."

"I can guess at your reasons why," he said. "But why don't you tell me?"

"Oh, let's start with the fact that we both have a closet full of loose ends. I don't think we need to add any more to our collection."

He crossed the room, stopping just behind her. She could smell the soft lift of his cologne, an intoxicating blend of lime and some ingredient she couldn't identify. She closed her eyes to bank its effect.

But then she felt his breath on her neck. His lips brushed the lobe of her ear, settled at the base of her throat. "Cole—"

"Okay," he said, retreating, even as he tipped her chin up so that she was forced to look at him.

"Here's the offer. There's somewhere I'd like you to go with me. Just for the day. If you still want to leave after we get back, I won't try to convince you otherwise."

"Where?" she asked, curiosity weakening her resolve.

"That part's a surprise. But I promise. You won't regret it."

She glanced at her open suitcase waiting on the bed. Then back to Cole's hopeful face. What else could she say but yes?

MARGO HAD SOMEHOW let herself be talked into a picnic on the beach with Harry.

Obviously, her platform of resistance needed a little fine-tuning. But she really had meant what she'd said last night. Harry had been more than clear with his intentions.

They sat on the sand under a giant umbrella, a blanket spread out in front of them with an assortment of food that would easily feed a party of eight.

"You actually talked the hotel restaurant into making fried chicken."

"Took some persuadin'," Harry said, "but no picnic's complete without it."

"That would be the Georgia boy in you," she said, unable to resist teasing him.

"Reckon so." He reached for the bowl and passed it to her.

She took out a piece, pulled off a small bite, the outer coat crispy and delicious. "Mmm."

"Glad you like it, ma'am," he said with a nod.

Along with the chicken, there were fluffy golden biscuits and mashed potatoes so good she could not resist a second helping. They washed it all down with a light white wine that tasted sharp and tangy and exactly right.

She took another sip and looked at Harry. "That was wonderful."

"We're not quite done yet," he said and pulled out a tin of cookies.

"Oh, I couldn't," she said, holding one hand to her stomach.

He took the lid off and waved them in front of her. "White chocolate macadamia nut."

"This is wicked, you know," she said, taking one.

"I specifically ordered them without calories."

"Oh, well, that settles it then." She took a bite of the cookie, closing her eyes and making a soft sound of approval. "That should be illegal."

"It probably is somewhere or other," he said, laughing.

She looked at him then, something warm and a

little alarming unfurling in the center of her chest. "I have a feeling you should be as well," she said with no idea how that note of flirtation had gotten in her voice.

"Really?"

"Really."

He reached across, made a gentle swiping motion on her chin with his thumb. "You have just a bit of cookie right there."

"Is it gone?"

"Almost," he said, his voice changing to velvet. "There's one more little piece," he added, leaning in until his mouth was mere inches away, "just here."

With that he brushed his lips across hers. Her eyes fluttered closed, and she willed him not to pull back.

And he didn't.

The kiss was as light as the landing of a butterfly, and still its effect on her completely devastating. She wondered how this was possible, and her mind veered off down the path of chemical explanation. Maybe that was what determined physical attraction, two similar makeups wandering around in search of each other until they eventually crossed paths and felt the pull like a magnet to steel. An old song with those exact words in the lyrics flitted through her head, and she thought maybe it didn't take a degree in physics to have figured this out.

He put one hand to the side of her face and deepened the kiss. There was sweetness there, not something she would have expected from a man who wasn't interested in taking the obvious anywhere past the obvious. All the same, it was there. The protective barrier she'd put in place last night proved worthless under this particular kind of assault, and she realized in a moment of clarity that she was in over her head.

"Margo."

Her father's voice penetrated the haze of pleasure clouding her brain. She sat up quickly, knocking over the cup of iced tea sitting on the quilt next to her. It flowed forward to be absorbed by the leg of Harry's swimming trunks. She jumped to her feet, grabbing a stack of napkins from the picnic basket and handing them to him. "I'm sorry."

"It's just tea," Harry returned, looking up at her father with a charming grin that clearly failed to charm him.

"I've been looking for you," her father said, dismissing Harry with a look. "I have the rental Jeep waiting at the back of the hotel."

"I thought we were meeting at three," she said, glancing at her watch to see that it was only one-thirty.

"There's a lot to see. I had hoped we could leave sooner than planned."

She glanced at Harry, then back at her father whose eyes snapped with disapproval. "All right," she said, brushing sand from her shorts and slipping her feet into her sandals. "Thank you for the lunch, Harry." This, she added without looking at him.

"Oh, you're quite welcome," he said in a voice that dripped amusement. "It was all my pleasure."

She could actually feel her father bristle. She took his arm and steered him toward the hotel.

"Margo, what are you doing with a man like that?" he asked in a stern voice.

She glanced over her shoulder. Harry was still watching them. It was clear from the look on his face that he'd heard the question. And she wasn't sure who she was angrier with. Her father for asking it. Or herself for not knowing the answer.

CHAPTER TWELVE

The eye never forgets what the heart has seen.—Bantu Proverb

COLE RENTED A Jeep from the hotel, and he and Kate drove into town to buy a few things. By the time he'd filled two buggies with fresh fruits and vegetables, a couple dozen boxes of cereal, cases of canned beans and tomatoes, a half dozen gallons of milk and a dozen packs of Oreo cookies, Kate looked at him as if he'd gone over the edge.

He wasn't willing to enlighten her just yet, so he shrugged and said, "You'll see," by way of explanation.

They drove away from town, up into the mountains. The road was narrow and curvy, the Jeep slowing to a crawl on a few of the hairpin turns. They'd left the top off, and the breeze caught Kate's blond hair, whipping it high about her face. He remembered how it had felt like silk in his hands last night.

They did very little talking throughout the drive, the silence between them comfortable, as if they'd known each other a long time. He couldn't explain this any more than he could explain what was happening to him where she was concerned.

Though he'd made this drive countless times in the past two years, he'd never taken anyone along with him. Actually, he'd never even told anyone that he'd been to this place. It was a secret of sorts, something he did to put himself in the middle of something that mattered.

He wasn't sure what it meant that he'd decided to bring Kate along today, although he would admit that it did mean something. More, he thought, than just a way to keep her from leaving. But if it did manage to accomplish that, he couldn't deny that he would be glad.

Thirty minutes or so after leaving town, he turned the vehicle onto a dirt road. Dust billowed up behind them. A couple of minutes later, the two-story stucco building appeared ahead. Groups of children played outside in the front yard, patches of grass interspersed with larger spots of dirt. One group appeared to be playing Red Rover, their dark skin glistening with the sweat of their enthusiasm, their smiles and laughter ringing out.

A small sign by the entrance gate read, Santa Maria Home For Children.

He cut the Jeep's engine and only then risked a look at Kate.

She stared at the children for a long time before she looked at him. "How do you know about this place?" she asked, her voice soft and low.

"When I first started coming to the island, I came across a little boy down near the marina one morning. He was going through the garbage cans looking for food. I learned later that his mother had died a few weeks before, and he had no other relatives. Their house was confiscated to pay for her medical bills, so he had nowhere to go. I started asking around and found out about this place. Scott Dillon, an American, started it ten years ago. He operates on a shoestring, but he does a lot of good."

"Wow," she said. "You do know how to surprise a girl."

"Come on," he said, getting out of the Jeep. "I'll introduce you."

She got out and followed him across the dirt parking lot to the area where the kids were playing. A couple of them spotted Cole and came running. Louis, now seven years old, launched himself at

Cole, arms clamping around his neck, legs locking around his waist.

"I didn't know you were coming," he said. Several of the other children threw themselves at him as well, and he was filled with the same warmth and gratitude he always felt when he came here.

"Will you give us piggyback rides, Cole?" Louis asked, pulling back to look at him with a wide grin on his face.

"Absolutely. First, I need to speak with Mr. Dillon and unload a few things we brought along. Then we'll get to the important stuff."

He let Louis slide to the ground, turning to find Kate lingering several yards away.

They walked back to the Jeep, gathered up a few of the bags and headed inside the building. Scott's office lay at the end of a short hallway. Cole set the bags down and knocked at the door.

"Come in," he called out.

Cole stuck his head inside. Scott sat behind a seen-better-days desk, what looked like a pile of bills spread out before him. He smiled immediately. "Cole," he said. "Come in, please."

"I've brought someone with me today," he said, stepping aside to beckon Kate forward. She walked into the office and stuck out her hand.

"I'm Kate Winthrop."

"Scott Dillon. I'm glad you could come with Cole."

Kate nodded once, her gaze taking in the small office, lingering on the photos covering the wall behind him. They were pictures of the children, playing, laughing, hugging, happy, sixty or more frames altogether. The first time Cole had seen them, he'd felt as if his eyes had been opened to something he'd never before been aware of. He could see from the look on Kate's face that the same was true for her.

"Please, sit," Scott said, waving a hand at the two chairs in front of his desk.

They sat down, and Scott began to ask about their trip.

"We had a little trouble with the boat," Cole said. "We're staying at the Ocean Breeze."

"Very nice," Scott said. "Is this your first trip to Tango Island, Kate?"

"Yes," she said. "It's beautiful."

"That it is. And impossible to forget once you've been here. I first came just over a decade ago and somehow never managed to leave."

"I can see why," Kate said. "Cole said you started the orphanage?"

He nodded and sat back in his chair, hands laced across his middle. "There was such a need," he said. "The island really has no social safety net, and during my first trip here, I discovered there were six-year-old children living completely on their own. It's amazing, actually, how well they managed to fend for themselves, but they needed a place to call home."

Kate glanced out the window where a group of children were playing tag. "How many children live here?"

"About thirty right now."

"Are they ever adopted?"

Scott sighed. "Rarely."

She nodded, obviously troubled by his answer. Cole wondered for a moment if he'd been wrong to bring her here. "We brought some supplies," he said. "We'd better get them out of the car."

"Thanks, Cole," Scott said. "I'll help."

The three of them walked back to the Jeep and gathered up the rest of the bags, then carried them to the orphanage kitchen. Two older women with dark skin and lined faces smiled at them, nodding their thanks for the food, then put it away.

They went back to the front of the building where Louis and the others greeted them with stored-up exuberance. They were immediately recruited into a game of dodgeball, and there was enough laughing and teasing to boost the most jaded of individuals.

At one point, Kate and Scott both declared

themselves in need of a break. They retired to the sidelines while Louis dragged Cole back out for more. And the truth was, he didn't mind at all.

KATE AND SCOTT sat on the low rock wall that stretched across one side of the playground. They were silent for a good bit, watching as Cole carted a clinging trio of boys from one end of the yard to the other, their giggles more than adequate proof of their happiness.

"How long have you known Cole?" Scott asked after a bit.

She smiled. "Not very long."

He lifted an eyebrow. "You're friends?"

"I think so." She realized how that must sound. But the truth was, right now, she wasn't really sure what they were.

He appeared to consider this, then said, "You must be good friends for him to bring you here. This place has been a comfort for him."

Keeping her gaze on Cole and the boys, she asked, "How so?"

"Maybe he feels that here his efforts matter," Scott said. "And they do."

"I can see that." With these boys, Cole was a different man from the one she'd seen to this point. Here, he held nothing back. She wondered if he'd been like that with his daughter. This open and caring.

"They are so pure, these children," Scott said. "I guess that's what drew me to them. They take what they are given with genuine gratitude and never expect or demand another thing."

"What did you do before you came here?" she asked.

"Oh, I was this corporate guy. Finally made it to the top after twenty years of grabbing and clawing. One day, I woke up to the realization that I would just as soon die as put in one more hour of that relentless grind. I bought a sailboat and pretty much let it pick its own course. We ended up here."

"You and Cole seem to have a lot in common."

"Yeah," he said. "I guess that's another one of our connections."

"Do you have a family?" she asked.

Scott let his gaze sweep across the playground. "They are my family."

After a while, Scott rejoined Cole for a round of piggyback rides. Kate stayed where she was, thinking about what he'd said. Of how fulfilling it must be to get up every day knowing that what you did would truly matter in the life of others.

Sitting there, she realized with a sudden wave of emptiness that this was missing in her own life.

She got up every morning to the same meaningless beat, wandering through the day with nothing more monumental to think about than her own need to avenge her ex-husband's betrayal.

The uselessness of this left a bitter, metallic taste in her mouth. She knew with a blinding clarity that she wanted her life to matter. She wanted to reach the end of her walk on this earth able to see that she had somehow made a difference. That her time here was not a complete waste.

She didn't know why Cole had brought her here, but she was so glad that he had. It felt as if a light had been switched on inside her, the darkness of all her doubts illuminated so that she could see them for what they were.

So she was not what her father wanted her to be. So she'd married a man who turned out to be a mistake. But she knew in the deepest part of her soul that from this day forward, she was going to take a different road. Find out what she had to offer. She'd once heard someone say the value of a life could be measured by whether a person had somehow made a difference in the world. If that was so, she had a lot of catching up to do.

THEY SPENT THE rest of the day playing with the children, even taking a group of six or seven of the older ones on a hike through the woods behind the orphanage. Cole was the engine, Kate the caboose. They wound their way through the dapples of sunlight that broke through the tall trees. By the time they reached the turnaround point where they sat in a circle and snacked on bananas and water, they were all sweaty and tired. They sat for a good while, telling stories and singing songs. Kate wanted to freeze their time there and keep it from slipping through her fingers.

Every now and then, she felt Cole's gaze on her. She was reluctant to look at him, maybe for fear that too much would show in her face. Things she wasn't sure she could even put a label on. When she finally let herself look up, he smiled. She smiled back, and it was amazing how something this simple could make her feel as if an entire world were opening up before her, a world she'd never even thought to imagine.

They were halfway back to the orphanage when Kate stumbled over a tree root and barely managed to catch herself before hitting the hard-packed dirt path.

Cole grabbed her arm. "Whoa, there."

"Graceful, huh?" she said.

"You okay?"

"Yeah. New feet and all."

He smiled again. Offered her his hand. For a moment, she wondered if he was just being kind, but then decided that even if he were, she didn't have it in her to decline his graciousness. She slipped her hand into his, and they walked the rest of the way back just like that.

CHAPTER THIRTEEN

One meets his destiny often in the road he takes to avoid it.—French Proverb

DRIVING AWAY FROM THE orphanage, Cole looked at Kate and said, "What did you think?"

"Where should I start?"

"Wherever you'd like," he said, steering the Jeep around a narrow curve.

"They're amazing."

"Yes, they are."

"Scott said there are few adoptions," she said, a note of sadness in her voice.

"Unfortunately."

"Can the children be adopted out of the country?"

"Actually, yes. It's just rare for anyone to inquire. And, too, most of the kids are older."

"Which increases the difficulty of finding families for them?"

He nodded.

"They're crazy about you," she said.

He lifted a shoulder. "That's just it. I'm nobody special, just willing to give them some time, and that's what they need."

She was quiet for a moment, and then said, "Have you ever thought about adopting?"

The question caught him off guard. Before he could answer, she said, "Oh. Cole. I'm sorry. That was unbelievably callous of me. I didn't mean to make it sound like you won't get your daughter back—"

"I know," he said. "You don't need to explain."

She leaned her head against the seat and sighed. "What I meant is that you obviously have what it takes to be a good father."

He managed a short laugh. "My ex-wife would have plenty to say about that assessment."

"What do you mean?"

He considered how to answer, and then went on, "I wasn't. A good father."

"I find that hard to believe based on what I saw today."

He kept his gaze on the road, seconds ticking by before he answered. "I would do it all differently now. That's why hindsight's such a valuable commodity."

"What would you do differently?" Kate asked, her voice gentle.

"That's the tricky part," he said. "Maybe I'd have to be a different person to actually do anything different from what I did. At the time, I thought I was doing the best I could."

"So who were you then?"

He ran a hand around the back of his neck. "I was one of six kids. Welfare mom. I think two of us had the same father. I grew up on Pop-Tarts and frozen pizza. That was at the beginning of the month. By the end of the month, we skipped a lot of meals. Our clothes came from biannual trips to the Salvation Army store. I remember Christmas as something to dread. Being the only kid in my class whose family didn't have a tree. I got my first job when I was twelve, saved everything I could manage to save and went to college on grants and scholarships. I wanted out of that life more than I could ever begin to describe to you. Once I saw that I could work my way out, I couldn't stop. It was like being given the golden key to another life. I put myself through college and then law school. Even after I got married, I took every case handed my way, worked all kinds of crazy hours. Basically, became an absentee husband and father."

He stopped there, unable to look at Kate, pretty sure of what he would see in her eyes if he did.

They'd driven a mile or more before she spoke. "You could have been describing my father just now."

"Yeah," he said. "I recognized myself when you told me about him."

They drove on for a while without speaking.

"I always thought of our relationship in black and white," Kate finally said. "He was wrong, and I was right. But I don't think it's possible for someone like me to know what it's like to grow up with nothing. I think I judged my father harshly. I wish I'd been more willing to see our differences through his eyes."

He pulled the Jeep over to the side of the road. They could see the lights of the town below and, in the distance, the ocean.

"Oh," Kate said. "It's incredible."

"It is," he said.

She leaned forward, elbows on her knees. "You completely changed your life, didn't you?"

"Too little, too late," he said.

"You'll find your daughter," Kate said softly, turning her head to look at him with intent eyes. "I know you will."

"I haven't let myself give up hope yet."

"Don't. She'll need you. Girls need their fathers."

The words were heartfelt, and he could see the chink in her armor. This vulnerable spot she had clearly spent a good portion of her life declaring indifference to. Something in her voice threaded its way through the center of him, and he felt a kind of tenderness for her that he hadn't felt for anyone in far too long.

He reached out to put his hand to the side of her face. She closed her eyes and made a soft sound of longing. From there, they fell into one another, mouths seeking and finding, as if they'd both been waiting for the moment. By now, there was familiarity in their kiss. In the not so distant past, this would have sent Cole running. Now, it drew him in, and he was weak to its pull.

They stopped for a second and looked at each other. Her eyes held questions that echoed his own. "I don't have any answers for where this is headed, Kate."

"I know," she said. "So maybe we ought to take it slow."

"Yeah," he said. "Slow."

They studied each other a while longer, and this time when he kissed her, he took his time with it. He felt like he was in high school again, hoping that she wouldn't find him somehow lacking on the comparison chart.

He wasn't sure how much time had passed when she pulled back, tucked her hair behind her ears and said, "Whew. If that's slow, my head is spinning."

"I think I'll take that as a positive," he said, leaning back to look at her.

"What?" she asked with a self-conscious laugh after he'd been staring for a few moments.

"You're a beautiful woman," he said.

She glanced down. "I'm sure you say that to all your vacation flings."

"Is that what this is?" he asked, attempting to keep the question light.

She looked up then. "I'm not the fling type. Although at the moment, I'm a little sorry to say so."

They both sat staring out at the town lights below them. Cole tried to think of something flip to say. Harry would have encouraged flip at this point. Things felt too serious. But somehow he wasn't feeling flip. He reached for her hand, entwining his fingers with hers. She squeezed. And he squeezed back.

THEY GOT BACK to the hotel around eight. Margo and her father were coming in from a walk on the beach when Kate and Cole pulled into the parking lot. Everyone was meeting for dinner at eight-thirty.

"I think I'll go take a quick shower first," Kate said.

"I'll turn in the Jeep," Cole said.

"Okay then. Thanks for a great day." She lifted a hand and took a step back, feeling awkward now.

"See ya at dinner," he said.

Kate walked back with Margo and her father. The professor talked about the shells they'd collected on their tour around the island that afternoon. She glanced at Margo, noticing the faraway look in her eyes, and wondered if she was thinking about Harry. They left the professor at his room to change for dinner, then walked to their own rooms a short stretch farther down the stone path.

"How was your day?" Margo asked.

"Unusual," she said.

"How so?"

"Can I tell you about it later?" she asked, suddenly aware that she wasn't ready to talk about it. Everything that had happened since that morning felt like a big puzzle in her head, a hundred different pieces that she hadn't yet figured out how to put together.

"Sure," Margo said.

"How about you and Harry? Did you do something today?"

Margo looked away. "We had a picnic earlier. Lyle and Lily said he left later to meet up with a friend."

"Really?" Kate asked, surprised.

She nodded. "Peyton something or other. I saw them in the lobby a few minutes ago. I think they must have once been something more than friends."

"Oh." Kate heard the disappointment in Margo's voice and wasn't sure what to say. *I'm sorry,* seemed more than a little lame, but she really was.

"It's okay," Margo said. "Let's face it, Kate. Harry and I are as different as two people could possibly be. He's this...rich playboy. And I'm, well...boring. I spent the afternoon listening to a dissertation from my father on why Harry is a horrible choice for me."

Kate put a hand on her shoulder. "First of all, Harry should be so lucky as to find a woman like you. And second of all, I think your father may not be able to be objective about anyone in your life."

Margo sighed. "I know. But I'm not the kind of woman who can be one in a lineup. And that's the kind of man Harry is."

Kate couldn't deny that she was right. Harry made little secret of his single-and-loving-it status. She gave this some consideration, then glanced at her watch. "So it would seem to me then that he just needs to have his eyes opened a little wider."

AT FIRST, MARGO proved to be a less than cooperative participant, making it clear she didn't want to try to be something she wasn't.

Kate assured her that wasn't going to happen.

They went to Kate's room where she steered Margo into the shower. There, she handed her a trio of her favorite shampoo, conditioner and gloss cream.

"They look expensive," Margo said.

"You deserve the pampering."

"There's no way you're ever going to make me look like her."

"That's not our goal."

"You didn't see her, Kate. She's like super-model material."

"Ah, but you have something she doesn't have."

"What?" Margo asked, skeptical.

"Harry's interest."

Once Margo was out of the shower and tucked into a fluffy white hotel robe, Kate placed her on a chair in front of a vanity mirror, squirting a dollop of thickening gel into the palm of her hand and then working it into her long hair. Next, she combed it out and reached for the blow dryer. Margo's hair had some natural curl to it, and Kate used a round brush to straighten it section by section. When she'd finished, it hung in a silky dark curtain down her back. Margo stared at herself in the mirror, eyes wide.

"Wow," she said. "How did you do that?"

"The magic of a good blow dry," Kate said. "And I'm not done yet."

She pulled out her makeup kit, reaching for a container of moisturizer. She smoothed a quarter-size dollop across Margo's forehead, cheeks and chin.

Next came foundation. Kate kept this light since Margo had good, clear skin. Then a light dusting of powder and a pink blusher. With a dark pencil, she etched in some color around the rim of her eyelashes and added a touch of mascara.

Again, Margo stared at herself in the mirror, a small smile tugging at the corners of her mouth.

"You like?" Kate asked.

"You're a magician," she said.

"A magician creates something out of thin air. I'm just working with what's already here."

Margo looked at her with appreciation in her eyes. "Thank you, Kate. You didn't have to do this."

"I want to do this," she said. "Come on. Now for clothes."

Fortunately, they were basically the same size. From her closet, Kate pulled a Donna Karan sleeveless wrap dress in light blue. She thought it would be perfect on Margo, and it was. They studied her reflection in the full length mirror, still the same Margo, only more chic and with an edge. She really was a lovely woman, and Kate wondered if she had subdued her beauty because of what happened to her when she was a child. It made sense that anyone who'd endured such a thing would be compelled to live unnoticed.

Strappy white sandals completed the outfit. Kate retrieved her jewelry case from the bathroom and pulled out a pair of diamond pendant earrings.

Margo held up a hand, refusing to take them. "I couldn't possibly wear those."

"I won't hear otherwise," she said.

"Really, Kate. It's too much."

"They're just earrings," she said, realizing the truth of this in a way she never had before. Not so long ago, she would have thought twice about risking their loss. Now their value seemed defined by the pleasure of sharing them with Margo.

She shook her head, and then said, "Thank you, Kate. I don't know what to say."

Once Margo had put the earrings on, Kate spritzed her with Chanel No. 5. She stepped behind her then, putting her hands on Margo's shoulders and turning her once more to the dressing mirror.

"Peyton, bring it on," Kate said.

And they both smiled.

WHEN THEY ARRIVED at the restaurant, everyone was already seated at the table.

Kate walked a step or two behind Margo, wanting her to have the floor. She immediately spotted Harry sitting at one end of the table, Cole on his right, a stunning blonde on his left. Kate and Margo took the two chairs at the opposite end, next to Lyle and Lily. She deliberately forged her way into the seat next to Dr. Sheldon. Margo didn't need her father's scrutiny just now.

The entire group sat in complete silence, staring at the two of them as if they had stepped off some unidentifiable spacecraft. It was exactly the response Kate had hoped for.

"My dear Margo," Lily said, one hand to her throat. "Why, look at you. You're positively stunning."

Margo placed her napkin on her lap, dropping her gaze. "Thank you, Lily. The credit—"

"—is all Margo's," Kate finished for her.

"Well, you look simply lovely tonight," Lyle said.

Margo returned the compliment. Lily waved a

hand at her fuchsia tunic. "Pish. There's not much you can do to rev up this old engine. The least I can do is send it out in hard-to-miss colors."

They all laughed, and Kate thought how nice it would be to arrive at Lyle and Lily's age with their insistence on making the best of whatever hand they were dealt.

She lifted her water glass to her lips, looking at Harry. He hadn't taken his eyes off Margo since they'd arrived at the table. "Harry," she said. "Aren't you going to introduce us to your friend?"

He cleared his throat, glancing at the girl-woman seated next to him, as if he'd forgotten all about her. "Oh. Yeah. This is—" He stopped there, blank for a moment.

"Peyton," Cole interjected with a grin.

"Hamilton," Harry said quickly, giving her a look of apology. "Peyton Hamilton."

"Hello, Peyton," Kate said. "What brings you to the island?"

"We're doing a photo shoot at one of the other hotels," she said, revealing a perfect white smile. "Just a short stay. Tomorrow, we're off to St. Barts."

"You're a model then?"

She nodded. "That's how Harry and I met. We used his boat for a *Cosmo* feature."

Kate could all but feel Margo wilting in her

chair. "It must be taxing to combine modeling with school," she said, unable to resist the jab at Harry.

"Oh, I'm not in school," Peyton said. "I gave that up at sixteen. It's like who needs it, you know?"

Kate glanced at Harry and smiled. "Of course."

Harry looked at Margo, and it wasn't hard to see him making the comparisons. For a moment, Kate almost felt sorry for Peyton.

"YOU ARE WICKED."

Kate turned to find Cole standing a few feet away from her, hands in the pockets of his jeans. Looking the slightest bit uncertain of his welcome.

"Hey, desperate measures," she said.

He walked across the sand and sat down beside her. "You definitely pulled out the big guns."

Several yards away, the ocean sent in another wave. It broke, dissipating in a swirl of foam. "Too much?" she asked.

"The opposite, I'd say. The last I heard, Harry was taking Peyton back to her hotel."

"Really?" Kate couldn't help smiling.

"Really." He hesitated for a moment, and then said, "I tried to catch up with you when you left the restaurant. What made you take off so fast?"

She pushed a hand through her hair, setting her gaze on the ink-dark horizon. It was hard to explain, when she wasn't sure of the answer herself. Sitting at the table with everyone telling stories and laughing, she'd felt drenched in loneliness. Why it had hit her there, surrounded by the people she had come to enjoy in the most unexpected ways, she didn't know. But then maybe it was exactly that. Once the trip ended, she would return to her other life, and she couldn't seem to find an ounce of joy in the prospect.

"I was just thinking about everything that happened today."

"And?"

She scooped a handful of sand, letting it sift through her fingers. "It's like a switch has been flipped inside me."

"In what way?"

She didn't answer for a moment, not sure what to say. She found it impossible to be anything other than honest with him. "This isn't easy to admit, but my life to date has pretty much been about me and very little else. Thinking about going back to that…I don't think I want to."

He stared at her for a long time. It was hard to read his expression in the faint light from the hotel, but she thought she saw something almost like respect there. Gratitude flared inside her. And at the same time, guilt. There was so much she hadn't told him. Somehow, she wanted to now. Part of her wanted to put it all out there and see if he still looked at her that way when she was done.

She tried not to think about how it had felt to kiss him earlier, which had exactly the opposite effect and sent memory flooding through her. The touch of his hand on her face. His mouth against hers. Warm and seeking.

She studied him now, his classically handsome face, his strong jaw and straight nose, the almost vulnerable tilt of his mouth.

Her chest felt suddenly tight, her breathing constricted.

He leaned in then and kissed her, and she realized he had been remembering as she had.

The sound of the ocean played around them like music. She could taste the salt of the ocean breeze on his lips. He pulled back after a bit, looking at her with the kind of raw need that literally made her heart race.

"I didn't expect you," he said.

"I didn't expect you, either."

It felt like one of those defining moments where they had to pick a direction. She didn't think there was any way to go back from here, forward or neutral the only options.

Just then, his cell phone rang. He pulled it from

the inside pocket of his jacket, flipped it open and said hello. He was quiet for a good bit, listening.

Kate moved away so that she couldn't hear the other person talking in case it was something private.

"I want to meet with him," Cole said. "Can you get him to wait until I get there?" From that point, he responded with single word answers, yes, no, okay. And thank you, before he hung up.

He stood with his back to her, staring out at the ocean.

"Is everything all right?" she asked.

He turned then, as if he had suddenly remembered her presence. "I think so."

She got up, brushing the sand from her legs and the back of her dress. "I should get back," she said, pointing to the hotel with the distinct feeling he would very much like to be alone.

He nodded once. "See you in the morning."

"Okay."

She slowly walked back to her room. She had no idea what that phone call had been about, but she did know one thing. If a door had opened between Cole and her today, that call had swung it shut again. Even now, she felt the slam reverberating through her.

CHAPTER FOURTEEN

*It does not matter how slowly you go so long
as you do not stop.*—Confucius

COLE COULD NOT deny he'd been an ass to Kate.

With Sam's call though, all the old feelings of
hope and disappointment had come flooding back.
He'd listened to what the man had to say, his heart
barely beating. It was as if everything around him
had dropped away, and there was only Sam's voice
in his ear.

He still couldn't quite bring himself to believe
it.

The deadbeat boyfriend had agreed to meet with
Sam tomorrow afternoon. Cole had asked Sam to
postpone the meeting until he could get there, but
Sam thought there was a very real possibility the
boyfriend wouldn't hang around that long. That
this might be the only opportunity. Cole didn't want
to take any chance on messing things up, even

though the little voice inside him kept reminding him of the other times he'd thought they were close to finding his daughter.

Sam was convinced this was the real deal though. He would call as soon as he and the ex exchanged money for Ginny's whereabouts.

He thought about Kate and how he'd let her go instead of explaining any of this. He owed her an apology.

He made his way along the stone path to her room and knocked with some hesitation. She answered after a few moments, dressed in a thick white hotel robe, her hair pulled back in a ponytail, her face shiny, as if she had just scrubbed it.

"Hey," he said.

"Hey."

"Could we talk for a minute?"

She glanced over her shoulder at the folded-down bed with its chocolates on the plump pillows. "Sure," she said, stepping out of the room and leaving the door slightly ajar.

They sat on the wood bench a few steps away. He felt unbelievably awkward, not sure where to start. "I'm sorry about—"

"You don't owe me an apology," she said, cutting him off.

"Yeah, I do," he said. "I shut you out. It's

something that kind of comes automatically to me. When things get difficult, I tend to hunker down and fight my way out instead of looking to someone else for support or comfort. Old habits, I guess."

She stuffed her hands into the pocket of her robe. "Are you all right?" she asked in a soft voice.

He wanted to say, yes, of course, he was. But the truth was, fear sat like a rock on his chest. "That call," he said. "It was from a private investigator. He's meeting with an ex-boyfriend of my wife tomorrow. He claims to know where they are. And for a price is willing to part with the information."

"Oh, Cole."

"Yeah," he said, letting out the breath he only now realized he'd been holding. "It's pretty big."

She said nothing for a few moments, then reached across and put her hand on top of his. "Shouldn't you go?"

"As soon as I hear from Sam. This isn't the first time we've thought we were close to finding her. The last time I flew to Seattle, and it turned out to be a case of mistaken identity. To be honest, I'm not sure my heart can take another disappointment like that."

She squeezed the back of his hand. "I don't know what to say."

"Words don't exactly cover it."

"No," she said. "They don't."

It was nice sitting here with her hand on his, a connection he very much needed. "Kate," he said after a bit. "About what was happening right before I got that call—"

"It's okay," she said, removing her hand from his to make a stop sign gesture. "You don't need to go there."

"That's just it," he said. "I'm not sure where we were going, but if we were going somewhere, could it wait until—"

"It can wait," she said, a gentle smile touching the corners of her mouth.

He picked up her hand and turned it over to rub the palm with his thumb. "A week ago, I would never have imagined this."

"Neither would I," she said.

"We'll figure it out?"

"We'll figure it out."

He leaned across and kissed her.

"Would you like to stay?" she asked, tipping her head toward the door to her room. "Just…stay. So you don't have to be alone tonight."

As soon as she said the word, a wash of relief and gratitude hit him. The thought of going back to his room and facing all his doubts and fears about finding Ginny was nearly unbearable. "Yes," he said. "I'd like to stay."

She stood and offered him her hand. He took it, and they walked back to the room, closing the door behind them.

HARRY LEFT PEYTON at the door of her bungalow just after 11:00 p.m. He wasn't sure who'd been more surprised by his departure, Peyton or him.

He walked back to the main lobby, feeling sullen and the slightest bit resentful. Two particular states that were completely atypical of his personality.

He'd always been a go-with-the-flow kind of guy. A few days ago, crossing paths with Peyton would have been a nice surprise, one he would no doubt have made the best of. Granted, she was a little younger than he was—okay, so a *lot* younger—but that had never bothered him before.

Tonight, he couldn't seem to get past noticing how often their conversation had veered toward MTV and the number of times she'd said dude in an average five sentences. As in, "Dude, are you actually turning me down?" This, just a few minutes ago as he'd walked away from her room.

So, what was the deal? He'd met a woman with an off the charts IQ, and suddenly he couldn't manage a modicum of interest in someone a little more average?

On the hotel veranda, he pulled up one of the

rockers, sat for a moment with his eyes closed, listening to the soft rush of the ocean.

At the sound of a familiar laugh, he looked up and spotted Margo headed his way with a dark-haired guy. He recognized him as one of the crew members on Peyton's photo shoot. Something that felt like acid started to burn in his chest. He considered getting up and walking in the other direction before she spotted him, but it was too late. She'd already looked his way, her smile faltering a moment and then righting itself like a preteen trying out high heels for the first time.

"Hey, Margo," he said, determined to be cordial.

"Hey, Harry," she said, smoothing a hand across the front of her dress, and then fluttering a wave at *GQ*-boy who was standing beside her. Harry didn't remember his name, but he was in his late twenties at best and New York cool. He probably took notes on the photo shoots. *Buy latest Moschino black T-shirt. Ultrahip. New Calvin Klein Jeans, too. Fit in extra weight workout at gym for increased bicep definition.*

"Harry, my man," *GQ*-boy said, offering him a high five which he met with the equivalent of a limp handshake. "Thought you were going out with Peyton."

"We called it an early night."

GQ-boy glanced at the Rolex on his left wrist. "I'll say. The night is young for a fox like you, Harry. There's got to be a henhouse open somewhere around here," he said, chuckling.

Harry, on the other hand, was not amused and didn't bother to pretend otherwise, even though he couldn't exactly accuse the guy of slander. He'd spent a good number of years carving out the reputation to which he referred and would even admit that not so long ago, he'd have found the comment funny, as well.

He glanced at Margo and wondered if it was possible to really change or if he was suffering from temporary infatuation with the idea of snagging a woman like her. And if that infatuation would fade like yesterday's news as soon as this trip ended.

"So, Margo," *GQ*-boy said. "How about that walk on the beach?"

"That sounds nice," she agreed without looking at Harry again.

"Sleep well, Harry," he added, taking her by the arm and steering her down the steps of the veranda. "Somebody's got to get some beauty rest around here."

For a moment, Harry saw himself going after the guy in a full-body tackle, rolling him through the sand until he no longer looked anything like a walking ad for Barneys Men's Store. Sanity prevailed, however, and he offered up a jovial wave, telling them to enjoy the full moon and not to worry about that silly island werewolf nonsense.

At this, Margo glanced back, a smile touching the corners of her mouth. Seeing that, a flag of hope went up inside him. And it seemed like a really important thing, the fact that he could make her smile.

On this, he walked to his room, down, but not beaten.

KATE AWOKE THE next morning to find Cole gone.

A feeling of emptiness settled inside her, and she wondered if it had been a mistake to bring him into her bed, innocent though it had been.

She'd always had trouble falling asleep at night. Even when it was late, and she was tired. Her mind refused to do a quick shut down, but rather replayed the events of the day, lingering over the ones that might have given cause for worry.

This hadn't been the case last night.

She remembered putting her head on Cole's shoulder, closing her eyes. And then waking to find him gone.

Clearly, she was setting herself up for a broken heart. But then she'd never thought she would feel anything like this.

Still wearing her thick terry cloth robe, she got out of bed and headed for the shower, thinking a few minutes of cold spray might give her the straight shot of logic she clearly needed.

Forty-five minutes later, she called Margo, and they agreed to meet for breakfast. Margo all but glowed as they took their chairs in the restaurant overlooking the ocean.

"So where did the evening end up?" Kate asked once the waiter had filled their white cups with coffee.

Margo picked up a small pitcher of cream, added some to her cup and stirred. "I took a walk on the beach with a nice guy working on Peyton's photo shoot."

Kate stared at her, surprised. "I thought you and Harry might have gotten together after dinner."

"Honestly? I think he would have liked to. He took Peyton home early."

"I heard. So why didn't you—"

Margo fiddled with her napkin. "I don't know, Kate. If I have to turn myself into something I'm not just to get Harry's attention, then that's just temporary. What's the point?"

"But Margo, that was you last night. We can be different versions of ourselves without changing who we are."

She took a sip of coffee, rubbing a thumb around the rim of the cup. "At the end of this trip, I'll go back to being Margo Sheldon, physics professor. And Harry will go back to being Harry Smith, woman chaser extraordinaire."

Kate wanted to disagree with her, but she couldn't bring herself to do so. Because what if Margo ended up being right? At least this way, she would have prepared herself so that losing him might be a little easier to bear.

She glanced up just then, spotting Cole and Harry in the doorway of the restaurant. Her heart did a little leap, and she realized then exactly how practical Margo's attitude really was. And that maybe she would do well to start subscribing to it herself.

Her gaze collided with Cole's, blowing her wise intentions of the previous few seconds to smithereens. It was as if a fog settled over her senses, making any danger to her well-being too fuzzy to bother with.

Harry waved, his uncertainty looking strange on him, like an ill-fitting jacket the likes of which he wouldn't be caught dead in. Both men walked over to the table. Harry said good morning. Kate jumped a little when Cole put his hand on her shoulder.

"Morning," he said.

"Hi," she managed, her voice sounding as if

she'd swallowed a handful of gravel. She cleared her throat, adding, "Have you eaten?"

"No," Cole said.

"Join us," she offered.

"I'm starving," Harry said, taking the seat next to Margo.

Without quite looking at him, Margo said, "The French toast is wonderful."

"That sounds perfect," Harry said, waving at a waitress. She came over, took his order and then looked at Cole who asked for coffee only.

Harry gave him a look. "How are you planning to run on that?"

"I'm not too hungry this morning," Cole said.

"That's a first," Harry said. "Anything wrong?"

"Just not hungry." The waitress came back to pour Cole's coffee. Once she moved to another table, he added, "I'll have the boat ready to go around eleven."

"Is everything fixed?" Kate asked, a little surprised to hear they were leaving this morning.

"Yeah," Cole said. "The mechanic called earlier and said it's good to go."

"Where are we going today?" Margo asked.

"I thought we'd do an excursion over to an un-inhabited island about an hour from here."

Harry leaned back and squinted. "If nobody lives there, what's the draw?"

"In the early nineteen hundreds, a small settlement of people lived on the island," Cole said. "A hurricane came through, and the tidal surge washed the entire population out to sea."

"How awful," Kate said, horrified by the image.

"And *why* exactly are we going there?" Harry asked, picking up his napkin so that the waitress could place his French toast in front of him.

"It's beautiful. Peaceful," Cole said.

"And morbid?" Harry added, drizzling syrup over his plate.

"I think it sounds fascinating," Margo said. "I'd like to see it."

Cole looked at Kate. "What about you?"

She studied him for a moment, aware of something different in his eyes and understanding that the explanation for it lay in this uninhabited island. "Sure," she said. "I'm along for the ride."

Cole took another sip of his coffee, nodding once and pushing back his chair. "Good. Can you guys make sure everyone knows to be at the pier by ten thirty or so?"

"Sure," they said in unison.

Harry shook his head once Cole was out of sight. "Why do I have the feeling we're getting ready to live out a *Scooby Doo* episode?"

Margo smiled. "And you're Shaggy?"

"Yeah," Harry said, "chattering teeth and all."

"As long as there aren't any hurricanes in the forecast," Kate said.

"That's the difference between today and a hundred years ago," Margo said. "People usually get some advance warning."

Kate wondered if she was talking about a lot more than hurricanes. She started to say she'd better go pack. But Margo slid back her chair and stood.

"I should go tell my dad we'll be leaving this morning. Catch up with you later," she said and left.

Harry watched her go, then looked at Kate. "Something I said?"

Kate considered how much to say, then decided the truth was the best route. "I think she's just plain scared of you, Harry."

"Of me?" he said, one hand to his chest.

"Of you."

"Why on earth would she be scared of me?"

She hesitated, considering how to answer. "Margo is a pretty serious woman. She's careful where she treads."

"And I'm a potential sinkhole?"

She tipped her head in response.

"This is ridiculous, anyway," he said, pushing back his plate. "You know, she's right. Saint and sinner, that's the two of us. And there's hardly anything compatible in that, is there? Besides, she's got her father. I don't think there's a man out there who could meet his approval."

"That's a little complicated, Harry."

"You mean a little weird, don't you? Is it normal for a woman her age to care so much what her father thinks?"

Clearly, Margo hadn't told him about what happened to her as a child. She wondered if it was her place to do so. But Harry looked so disgusted, so miserable, that she decided maybe it was the right thing. And so she told it as Margo had told her, matter of fact.

Harry's face blanched to the white of the cloth on their table. "My God. You mean no one knew where she was for three years?"

She shook her head. "I guess her father had to assume she was dead. Can you imagine?"

"No," he said, his voice quiet with disbelief. "No."

"I admit I had the same thoughts about his being so overprotective, but I think I can understand now."

"Yeah, I guess so. Wow."

"She looks strong, Harry," she said carefully. "But maybe there's a part of her that's fragile and unwilling to risk pain."

He looked at her for a moment, then said, "Thanks for telling me. You probably saved me from being a real idiot."

He stood then and left the restaurant before she could ask what he meant by that.

BY ELEVEN-FIFTEEN, they were headed across open water. Cole stood at the wheel and double-checked the satellite phone he used when cell reception was questionable. Harry entertained everyone with made-up ghost stories that got more unbelievable with every twist judging from the tolerant smiles on the faces of his audience.

Cole and Kate had been doing the avoidance dance again this morning. He couldn't deny that he was leading. He knew what she must be thinking. That he regretted the fact that they'd slept together last night. But it wasn't that. It was the opposite, actually.

She was the only one who knew what he faced today. He felt as if an axe hung over his head. If it fell, he'd be permanently split in half. And he wasn't up to seeing the reflection of that awareness in her face.

An hour after they set out, he spotted the island in the distance, slowing the boat as they got closer. A hundred yards off shore, he brought it to a stop and lowered the anchor. Harry dropped the dinghy to take in to the beach. Cole passed out life jackets for everyone and then headed below to retrieve the cooler of picnic lunches he'd asked the hotel to put together that morning.

Halfway there, he heard Kate call out behind him. He turned and watched her descend the stairs to stop in front of him.

She stared at him for a moment, looking uncertain. "Are you all right?"

"Yeah," he said. "Just not very good company."

"You don't have to be."

He could see that she meant it, and he suddenly felt like the world's biggest jerk for shutting her out. "I'm sorry for leaving this morning without saying anything."

"Don't be," she said. "I can't imagine how you must be feeling. If it's easier to kind of hang out by yourself, I understand. I just wanted you to know I'm here if you don't want to be alone."

"Thanks," he said. Looking at her, an emotion something very like tenderness swept up through him. This, too, was a feeling he hadn't known in some time. It caught him off guard, and he couldn't think of a single thing to say in response.

A noise sounded behind them, a crash of some kind, followed by a startled yelp.

"What was that?" Kate asked.

"I have no idea," he said. He pointed toward the galley and put a finger to his lips. Silent, they walked to the door. He turned the knob and slowly opened it. Then stopped and stared.

From behind him, Kate said, "Oh, my goodness."

On the floor, amidst a pile of brooms and mops, sat Louis.

"Are you all right?" Cole asked, extending a hand to pull him up.

The boy's nod was sheepish. "I'm sorry about the mess, Mr. Hunter."

"Louis," he said, trying to make his voice stern. "What are you doing here?"

"One of the older guys at the home said you probably wouldn't ever come back again."

Cole heard the worry in the boy's voice and realized he'd never understood quite what his visits to the orphanage meant. "Does Mr. Dillon know you're here?" he asked in a soft voice.

Louis shook his head, looking down at the floor with a guilty expression.

Kate started picking up the items that had fallen out of the closet.

"How did you get in here?" Cole asked.

"I waited until the guys at the pier weren't looking, and then I sneaked on."

For a few moments, Cole had no idea what to say. "Scott must be worried sick about you," he finally managed.

"I'm sorry," he said in a small voice.

"We'll have to get you back."

Louis nodded.

Kate placed the last mop in the closet, then looked at Cole. "Could he go with us to the island first?"

Louis turned molten eyes to him, the plea there too plain to ignore. How could he say no? "Louis, what you did was wrong for a lot of reasons. You can stay until this afternoon, but only if you call Mr. Dillon and let him know where you are. You can tell him we'll have you back later today."

Louis's relief was nearly palpable. "Yes, sir."

Kate put a hand on his shoulder, looking at Cole with gratitude. The three of them headed upstairs then where he introduced Louis to everyone and explained that they would be taking him back to Tango Island when they left here. He searched for Scott's number in his directory, then dialed and handed Louis the phone.

He walked over to stand by the railing, talked for a couple of minutes and then came back and handed the phone to Cole. "He's pretty upset."

Cole gave the boy's shoulder a squeeze before

saying, "It'll be all right. He's just worried about you. You can't just take off without telling anyone where you're going."

Louis nodded and looked down at his feet. "I won't do it again."

Cole glanced at the phone, noticing that he had a message. He walked over to the other side of the boat and punched in his password. It was Sam, apologetic. "Cole, the ex changed the meeting time to four this afternoon. I'll call you as soon as I know something."

He clicked off the phone, resisting the impulse to hurl it over the side of the boat. He heard footsteps behind him. "Everything all right?" Kate asked.

"Yeah," he said, hearing the lie in his own voice.

She put a hand on his arm. "You don't look like it's okay."

He started to say something, but the words stuck in his throat.

"You don't need to explain," Kate said. "I'll get a life jacket for Louis."

He nodded and then decided that the only way to get through this day was to close out all the scenarios of failure that kept looping through his head and let himself believe that this time he would find his daughter.

CHAPTER FIFTEEN

He who is a slave of truth is a free man.
—Arabian Proverb

KATE FOUND LOUIS to be nothing short of a delight.

In his eyes, this was clearly an adventure of the highest magnitude. Watching him, she decided that she would let herself see this day as he saw it. A step outside of the ordinary. She had begun to realize that she wanted to be the kind of person who could see the little surprises in life as added bonuses rather than as problems to solve.

Louis was an added bonus.

Cole transported the group in two trips from the *Ginny* to the white sand shore of their deserted island. Lyle, Lily and Kate went with Louis on the first ride, stepping onto the beach with exclamations of delight while Cole went back to get the others.

From the shore, there was no sign that humans had ever lived on the island. No buildings of any kind. Just an indefinite stretch of white sand and aqua water.

Lyle and Lily spread their towels beneath a palm tree, while Kate and Louis started a sand castle, using a couple of the red plastic cups she pulled from her beach bag. They'd just finished the moat when Cole arrived with Harry, Margo and her father. Lyle and Lily waved Dr. Sheldon their way, insisting that he take the extra towel they'd set up and then immediately peppering him with questions about the students he'd taught over the years and what they'd gone on to do.

Cole beached the dinghy, then made his way over to where Kate and Louis were now forming the foundation of their castle.

"Impressive," he said.

"Join us," she offered.

"It's going to be huge," Louis said.

"Then maybe you do need a little help," Cole agreed, dropping onto the sand beside them.

They all worked for a while without talking. Kate finished up the moat by adding a couple of offshoots. Cole and Louis completed the base of the castle, then got busy with the second level. When they'd finished, it was four stories high, the top a Rapunzel-type tower.

Louis headed for the ocean, running back and forth for cups of water until the moat was full.

Kate got up from the sand, walking a short distance away to where a stand of flowers grew in a raucous profusion of yellow and orange. She picked a few and carried them back to the castle. "Since we're short on damsels in distress," she said, "the place needs some flowers."

Louis watched her stick one in each of the holes they'd carved for windows, then smiled.

"A woman's touch," Cole said.

She glanced up at him, flushing at the way he said this. It occurred to her that just a few days ago, there would have been sarcasm in his voice. She liked the fact that there was none there now.

Just after noon, they made a picnic spot in the shade of a couple of palm trees, pulling food from the coolers they'd brought ashore. Louis ate with the kind of intent that said too clearly how many meals he had missed in his young life. A knot formed in her heart, and the taste of her own sandwich dulled under the realization.

When everyone had finished, they put the leftover food back in the coolers. Cole suggested a walk to the other side of the island where the stone huts occupied by the people who had once lived there still stood.

They all agreed to go, even Dr. Sheldon, who offered a chivalrous arm to both Lyle and Lily. The walk took a half hour or so, and the sounds they made against the island's stillness were happy sounds, filled with laughter and teasing. At one point, Harry told another of his famous ghost stories, his rendition more silly than scary. Even so, Louis reached for Kate's hand, and they walked the rest of the way like that. It felt good to be needed, even in as slight a way as this.

They rounded a bend in the beach to find a cluster of a dozen or so stone huts, still complete except for their missing roofs.

"It's kind of eerie," she said, rubbing her arms against a sudden chill.

"Did people used to live here?" Louis asked.

"Yes," Cole said.

"Is this the island where the people were all killed by a hurricane?"

Cole nodded. Louis ran to one of the buildings, putting a hand on the rock, as if to make sure it was really there. Harry and Margo walked over and said something to Louis. Harry took the boy's hand, and they weaved their way through the small village.

Kate and Cole sat on an enormous boulder that looked as if it might have once marked some kind of entrance. The sun slipped behind a cloud, and she flipped her sunglasses to the top of her head. "How horrible that an entire town full of people could just be swept away," she said.

Cole didn't answer for a few moments, and when he did, his voice had a faraway note to it. "Isn't that how it happens in life, though? One minute, the sun is shining, and everything seems good. The next, the world is no longer recognizable."

She heard the weight in his voice, wished she could say something that might lift it. "You mean Ginny?"

He looked at her, the pain in his eyes undeniable. "When you're living your life a certain way, it seems normal. I thought I was normal. That it was the right thing for me to get out there with my swing blade every day cutting a path to a secure future. I would give anything to go back and change who I was."

"What would you change?" she asked, her voice low.

"The way I saw what I had," he said without hesitation. "I think of my daughter and how days would go by when I would leave the house before she woke up and she would be asleep when I got home." He shook his head. "What was I thinking? How could I have thought anything could be more important than her?"

"Cole—"

He held up a hand. "I didn't tell you this so you could try to make me feel better. I screwed up, and I have no one to blame for it but myself."

There was so much she would have liked to say, but didn't. She knew he didn't want to hear it, that accepting responsibility for his choices was part of how he would eventually heal. She thought of her own life, her own choices, and knew she'd reached the fork in the road. In one direction was the way she used to live, hand outstretched for all she believed was hers for the taking. In the other, a new life, a clear vision of another Kate. A Kate that might look for some way to give back instead of take.

Louis reappeared with Harry and Margo, Harry doing what appeared to be the Michael Jackson moonwalk. Louis smiled, happiness changing his face, his whole posture. Watching them, something lightened inside her, and she was certain of one thing. Like Cole, she didn't want to go back to who she'd been. Never considering how children might fit into her life. She wanted to be the kind of person who could give a boy like Louis a reason to smile.

It was a lofty enough goal for a girl who not so long ago had never thought to care.

WHEN HARRY ASKED Margo if she'd like to look around the island, her first inclination was to say no.

There seemed little point in continuing their game of flirt and withdraw. But as she'd already acknowledged, she had a difficult time turning Harry down.

So here they were, walking alone now, after leaving Cole, Kate and that precious Louis in the middle of what must have once been the island's population center. They followed a path to a stretch of pristine white beach. The turquoise water folded its way in from the ocean, breaking onto the sand in gentle waves.

Harry took off his shoes and waded in, looking back to beckon her forward. She hesitated, then slipped off her sandals and joined him. They stood, silent, staring out at the bare horizon.

"Could there be anything more beautiful?" she asked.

From the corner of her eye, she saw him turn to look at her. In a moment of awkwardness, she wondered if he might think she'd staged the question, hoping for a cliché answer from him. Her face heated with the thought, and she struggled for some other thread of conversation to initiate.

Her mind went blank, however, when he put a hand on her arm and turned her to face him. He stepped forward, the water splashing against their legs. He looked down at her for a long time, as if memorizing her face. "Yes," he said. "You."

She knew better than to let herself be swayed by pretty words, but swayed she was.

He reached out, touched her face with the back of his hand. "Kate told me about what happened when you were a child."

He said it so softly that she thought for a moment she might not have heard him. Sympathy tinted his voice, but also deep caring, and it was this which made tears spring to her eyes. She couldn't remember the last time she'd cried about it. She tried hard not to now, but failed.

Harry pulled her into his arms, enclosing her in the tight circle of his embrace. She felt utterly safe there, safe as she had once felt a long time ago, before that black time in her life. He took her hand and led her along the beach until they came to a spot of shade beneath a lone palm tree. They sat down, and still he didn't let go of her hand, rubbing the back of it with his thumb.

For a long time, they didn't say anything. Finally, Harry said, "I can't imagine how you survived that."

"I lived on hope," she said. "I prayed every day that someone would tell my father where I was. And one day, that's exactly what happened."

His arms tightened around her. "How do you ever look at life the same way again?"

"You don't," she said simply. "It affected my father more than it did me. Permanently, I mean."

"Yeah. I think I understand that a whole lot better now. I can see why he would never want to let you out of his sight."

"And yet I'm thirty-five years old. I guess it's not healthy for either of us. During the time I was gone, he had a nervous breakdown. Everyone thinks I'm the fragile one, but that's not true, really."

'That's an awfully big sack of responsibility for you to be carrying around," Harry said, rubbing her shoulder now.

Raw response skittered through her, and she closed her eyes to focus on what he'd said. "I guess I do feel responsible in a way. I knew not to talk to strangers, and yet I let myself be fooled."

"Margo. Children are innocent. Adults have weapons like cunning and evil. How can innocence stand a chance against either of those?"

He leaned back a bit, turning her face to his. He studied her for a while, and she was aware of the sound of the waves, the feel of the sand where they sat. Mostly, though, she was aware of Harry. The way he smelled, the depth of feeling reflected in his blue eyes. He leaned down and kissed her. She thought for a moment of resisting, but as quickly as it appeared, the impulse was gone. Harry was safety. She knew this with a certainty that settled on her like the warmth of a down quilt on a cold winter night.

She lay back on the sand, Harry above her now. They looked at each other for a long time, no words necessary. He lowered his head and kissed her again. And she thought if they stayed right there for the rest of her life, it would be just fine with her.

THEY SPENT THE next couple of hours exploring the island. Cole saw it through Louis's eyes, aware that he had failed to ever see the world through his daughter's eyes. The regret of this sat like a stone on his shoulders, and he swore to himself that if he were given another chance, he would be a good father. He would be a better man.

They'd split off into three groups, Harry and Margo disappearing altogether, the professor and the Granger sisters meandering along the water's edge, picking up shells. Cole, Kate and Louis ventured toward the center of the island, coming across a flat of rock on which a dozen or so iguanas lazed in the afternoon sun.

"Wow," Louis said. "Can I pet one of them?"

"I doubt they'll let you," Cole said.

"I'll be real easy."

Cole and Kate watched the boy tiptoe across the

sandy ground, squatting a couple of feet back from one of the larger creatures.

"When I was a little girl," Kate said, "I wanted to adopt a baby when I grew up. One of my teachers adopted a little boy who was four or five years old. He'd been in an awful situation, a mother on drugs who'd abandoned him. A neighbor found him after a few days. I remember the bond between him and his adoptive mother. It was amazing to see how much they loved each other. It was like they both needed one another on some deeper than normal level. Do you think that's what real love is?"

"Maybe the lasting kind," he said.

She watched Louis, and Cole saw something soften in her eyes. "These last few days I've realized some things about my life."

"Like what?"

"That I've had my compass pointed everywhere except true north. That I'm only just now realizing I didn't have any idea where that was."

"And now you do?" he asked.

She lifted her gaze, looking at him for a long moment, before saying, "I'm beginning to."

And with those three words, he felt something shift inside him. The blooming of something he'd never expected to feel. But it was real. He couldn't deny it. More amazing still, he didn't want to.

He reached out and took her hand in his. And it was nice, this connection. It felt as if someone had taken a sledgehammer to the walls he'd built around himself these last two years. They tumbled to the ground, piece by piece, until he was left standing without an ounce of protection against what was happening between them. In place of all his previous suspicion, doubt and contempt loomed a single feeling.

Trust.

LOUIS CALLED OUT to Cole, waving him over to the rocks where the iguanas hadn't bothered to leave their sunning spot. Cole let go of Kate's hand, leaving her with a look that caused something in the middle of her chest to flip right over.

She watched him walk away, something like terror settling in behind her euphoria. It scared her, what was happening between Cole and her. On several different levels.

But the main one being that she hadn't come clean with him. She thought about the suitcase full of money hidden in her cabin and wished she'd never found it. Wished she'd closed the door on the mistakes she'd made with Karl and just left it at that.

Instead, she'd created a situation that could only

end in confrontation. Karl was not a man to give up on anything that involved money. She should know this better than anyone.

She watched Cole squat down beside Louis, one hand on the boy's shoulder. And suddenly, everything between Karl and her felt icky and repulsive. She wanted no part of it. Wished she had simply taken the money to the police and left it up to someone else to bring Karl to his knees. She decided now that this was what she must do. Go home and tie up her loose ends. She couldn't let herself begin something with Cole until she did.

Cole and Louis headed her way, Louis talking non-stop. Cole took her hand again, and they headed back the way they came. Despite the resolution she'd just made, she loved this simple connection between them, her hand in his, her happiness mingled with guilt though it was.

They were halfway back to the spot where they'd come ashore when Cole's phone rang. He let go of her hand and pulled it from his pocket with a quick jerk. "Hello."

He said nothing for a minute or more, and then asked, "Are you sure?" The thread of urgency in his voice was unmistakable. Kate's heart began to pound, and she said a silent prayer that this would be the news he had been waiting for.

A few more seconds passed before he said, "I'll be there as soon as I can." He flipped the phone shut, then turned to her with a smile. "He found her."

"Oh, Cole. How wonderful."

"We should go," he said. "I'll need to arrange a flight."

He walked over and put his arm around her shoulders, pulling her against him so that her face was pressed to his chest. She breathed in the warm, comforting scent of him, and there was no place in the world she would rather have been.

THEY ARRIVED BACK at their picnic spot to find the rest of the group already there. They all wore worried expressions, and their gazes settled heavily on Kate.

She felt a flicker of unease, looking at Harry who said, "The boat is gone. This note was pinned under one of the cooler lids."

He handed it to Cole who read it, then looked at her. She saw it clearly, the curtain drawing shut over his eyes. A sick feeling swept through her. She took the note.

Guess you won't have the last laugh after all, huh, Kate? Enjoy the island scenery.

Karl

She glanced out at the spot where the boat had been. "Oh, no," she said, one hand to her mouth.

"What is this, Kate?" Cole asked, his voice even.

She couldn't answer for a few moments, and when she did, the words had no more weight to them than a cold, limp dishrag. "I'm sorry. I'm so sorry."

Cole pinned her gaze with his. "Maybe it's time you explained what for."

CHAPTER SIXTEEN

A truth spoken before its time is dangerous.
—Greek Proverb

THIS COULDN'T BE happening. Cole's pulse jumped in his throat, and he forced himself not to say anything until they were out of earshot of everyone, including Louis who was with Lyle and Lily.

He waited until they rounded a bend in the beach, before turning to Kate. "This has something to do with the two break-ins on the boat, doesn't it?"

Kate bit at her lower lip, folding her arms across her chest. "I don't know for sure."

"But you suspect it does?"

"Before this, I really didn't think either incident had anything to do with me. Now, I—"

"Now you what, Kate?" The words came out fast and harsh. Anger had pulled a red haze over his vision. "I thought you were being straight with me. I thought you were someone I could—"

"Cole, don't."

"I was right, after all, wasn't I? You *were* hiding something on my boat."

"I should have told you," she said, regret etched in her voice.

"Told me what?" He heard the iciness in the question and wondered what craziness had ever made him think he knew her well enough to trust her. This was a lesson he had learned two years ago from his own wife, a woman he thought he knew completely. Who as it turned out, he hadn't known very well at all. "Told me what?" he repeated.

"It's complicated," she said.

"I don't exactly have anywhere to go."

The barb hit its intended target. She winced. "Karl. My ex-husband. I kind of took back some money that he—"

"This is about money?" The words came out as a small explosion.

"It's not the way it sounds," she said.

"Let me see if I've got this right. That bag you brought with you on the boat. That's where the money was, right?"

"Cole—"

"And Karl or someone representing Karl came looking for it and took my boat as an added bonus?"

"Please, Cole. Listen—"

He started backing up. "I don't need to listen. I think I know just about everything I need to know." He turned then and headed back down the beach, not sure which emotion would win out. Anger, disgust or disappointment.

THE THOUGHT OF following Cole back to where the others waited sent a wave of nausea over Kate. These people had come to mean something to her, and she'd let them down. There was no other way to see it. How could she expect them to feel anything but contempt for her?

She felt contempt for herself.

Strangely enough, she wasn't even angry with Karl. She'd known what he was capable of. And she'd let this happen.

She grappled for some piece of rationalization, but her umbrella of excuses was now full of holes. Useless, really. And so she started down the beach under a downpour of regret.

Cole was on the phone when she reached the group. His back was turned to her, but everyone else looked straight at her. She hung for a moment between the desire to turn and run and an over-whelming need to beg their forgiveness. She started to say something, and it was then that Margo held out her hand. Kate reached for it with tears in her eyes, gratitude a lump in her throat. But Louis tied a simple knot in her heart when he came over and took her other hand. She could see that he had no idea what any of this was about, his only desire to offer comfort. And she promised herself she would take a lesson from this.

From some distant memory came a picture of herself sitting in church with her father, listening as the pastor explained the definition of grace. For some reason, she had never quite grasped the true meaning of the word. It was only now with forgiveness flowing from the touch of these new friends that it became clear to her what it felt like to be forgiven for something, even when forgiveness was completely undeserved.

She glanced at Cole who had flipped his phone closed, but still stood staring out at the ocean, as if he might find some measure of calm there. At his feet were the remnants of their sand castle, the tide having washed the biggest part of it away. He turned after a moment, addressing the seven of them without letting his gaze intersect with hers.

"I spoke with a patrol boat from Tango Island. They're sending someone out to pick us up. They also have a helicopter searching for the *Ginny*. Someone should be here in an hour or so."

Relief cascaded over her, a waterfall of gratitude

that they would not be forced to spend the night here without food or water because of her. Everyone spoke at once, the same relief apparent in the chorus of voices. "That's great! No big deal then."

As soon as it was quiet again, she felt compelled to offer an explanation, even though she dreaded seeing in their eyes what she had seen in Cole's. "This is my fault," she said, glancing down at her hands. "Dirty laundry from my divorce, I'm afraid. Something I should never have risked affecting any of you. I'm so sorry that it has. I'm so sorry—"

They gathered around her without letting her finish, a mini cheering squad, when a firing squad might have been more appropriate. Harry gave her a big hug, Margo next, Lyle and Lily patting her cheeks with reassuring clucks of "Don't worry, dear. Everything will be fine."

Even Dr. Sheldon gave her an awkward pat on the back and said, "We all make mistakes."

Louis wedged himself into the circle and said, "I wouldn't mind being stuck here for a while. I could almost pretend I didn't have to go back."

Tears burned in her throat. She couldn't help it. She reached for Louis's hand and gave it a squeeze. From the corner of her eye, she saw Cole watching them. But for the life of her, she couldn't bring herself to look at him. She had—without question—derailed any feelings that might have been developing between them. In his face, she knew she would see proof of this. She would pass on that just now.

SINCE THEY'D BEEN assured of rescue, everyone began to enjoy the island again. Louis and Margo built a new sand castle.

Kate sat a few yards away, and Harry came over to sit down next to her. "He'll get over it, you know."

She made a sound that fell somewhere between a laugh and a sob. "I'm not sure this is the kind of thing a person can get over."

"Sure, it is."

"He's waited all this time to find his daughter, and now, because of me, he's stuck here."

"A minor waylay," Harry said. "A ripple in the big picture."

"You don't know that. What if he doesn't get there in time? What if his ex-wife finds out he knows where she is and takes off again?"

"Those are some awfully big what-ifs."

"Not that unlikely, though. I should have known something like this would happen."

"Crystal ball got a little cloudy, huh?" Harry said, a notch of amusement in his voice.

"How can you find anything funny in this?" she asked, resting her chin on her knees and staring out at the sea.

"It's kind of a rule I live by. Look for the lighter side. Kate, no one here thinks you meant for this to happen."

She glanced at Cole, now helping Louis. The worry lines in his face had lightened, and she realized Louis had that effect on him.

"Not even Cole," Harry said. "He might have been a little mad at first, but see, even now the fog's started to lift."

"I lied to him," she said. "I don't think he'll get over that."

Harry was quiet for a few moments, and then said, "Sometimes we make the wrong choices for the right reasons, Kate. You're not a bad person. Although I suspect that's not what you think. Don't let this be your convicting piece of evidence. It won't hold up in court. I've seen enough proof to the contrary."

"Thank you, Harry."

"You're welcome," he said. "And besides, I should be thanking you."

"For what?"

"For giving me a more complete picture of Margo. She's an extraordinary woman."

"Yes, she is," she said, pleased by the sincerity in his voice. "Just be careful with her."

"I intend to," he said. "And you be careful with you."

Just then a boat appeared on the horizon, a loud horn sounding in the distance. "The cavalry," she said, grateful for Harry's faith in her, unsubstantiated though it might be.

"Forward, ho," Harry said, standing and offering her a hand. "Hope they've got some food on that boat. I'm starving."

Margo walked over, slipped her arm through his. "Understandably. You've gone what, four hours without eating?"

"Possibility stress. Very taxing on the body to think about missing a meal."

"Ah," Margo said. "There's one for the talk show hosts."

Kate listened to their easy banter and felt an undeniable spike of wistfulness for what had developed between them. Earned though Cole's rejection most certainly was, it still stung.

Actually, it hurt.

A lot.

COLE WASN'T SURE how he was supposed to act.

He looked at Kate and wondered if she were

anything like the person he'd imagined her to be. As it turned out, he was missing several major pieces of the puzzle, and the hard to accept part was that she'd left them out intentionally. When he fit them into the picture, she didn't look anything like the Kate he'd shared a bed with last night.

That Kate was vulnerable-Kate. Starting-all-over-Kate. This Kate…he didn't know who she was.

The patrol boat sped across the stretch of ocean toward them. They'd put the word out about his missing boat, although it hadn't been found yet.

"Hey."

He turned to find her looking at him with uncertainty clouding her eyes. For a moment, something inside him gave, and he wished he could turn the dial back to that morning when pretty much anything had seemed possible for them. "Hey," he said.

"Cole." She stopped, taking a deep breath as if reaching for some way to explain. "I never meant for this to happen."

"What did you think would happen?"

"I thought I would give Karl time to cool off. And then I would go home and force him to own up to what he'd taken from me."

"Which was?"

"Just about everything my father left me."

"And you were willing to put everyone on this trip at risk?"

"I didn't think of it that way."

"But isn't that how it turned out?"

She glanced away, then looked back at him. "I'm sorry."

"What's done is done." He was being a jerk. He knew it, and yet he couldn't seem to help himself.

Her eyes widened, and then she blinked away her surprise, as if she'd expected it. "I can take Louis back to the orphanage," she offered.

"Thanks. I appreciate it," he said, keeping his voice neutral. "Tell Scott I'll give him a call."

"I will." She nodded once, then turned and headed for the other side of the boat where Margo and the Granger sisters had been doing a less than convincing job of ignoring them. He started to call her back, the words nearly automatic, but then he stopped himself. What good would it do?

If he'd learned anything from these past two years of searching for Ginny, it was that wanting something to be different didn't make it so. Reality was a painful pill to swallow. And the reality of Kate and him was this: a beginning that started with deceit could only end one way.

ONCE THEY REACHED Tango Island, Cole explained that Harry would be taking over the rest of the trip for him. They would wait there overnight to see if the boat was found. If not, they could finish out their vacation on the island or return home with a full refund.

It was a motley crew that boarded the open-sided island taxi waiting at the end of the pier. They had no luggage, no belongings. Cole had arranged with the hotel to extend credit until the situation had been further resolved.

They were all about to get on the truck when Kate realized Cole wasn't going with them. He hugged Lyle, Lily and Margo, then shook hands with Dr. Sheldon. He said something to Harry, then stepped back to where she stood next to Louis. He put a hand on the boy's shoulder and told him he would see him soon. Louis nodded, his lower lip trembling.

Cole leaned in and gave him a hug. "No more running away, okay?"

"Okay," Louis agreed, eyes downcast.

Cole looked at her then, and several long seconds passed before either of them spoke. And then it was at the same time.

"I'm sorry," she said.

"Be careful," he said.

She hadn't expected this. She couldn't imagine

that he would care at this point what happened
to her.

She nodded once, hard, tears stinging the back
of her throat. "Good luck. I hope you find her."

Once they were all seated the taxi pulled away.
Everyone waved and called out goodbye to him. She
sat with her hands on her lap, not trusting her voice.
And even when he turned his back and began to walk
away, she didn't take her eyes off him until the taxi
rounded a corner, and he disappeared from her sight.

THEY CHECKED INTO the hotel, and she actually got
her old room again. She called Scott first thing. He
said he would come down and get Louis, but she
asked if the boy could stay with her for the night.
She would bring him back in the morning. Scott
agreed, and she was surprised when he didn't ask
if Cole would be coming. She wondered if he'd
already called and explained what had happened.

She promised Louis a trip to the pool as soon as
she made one last phone call. This one to Tyler, who
took her call with an air of resignation, as if he had
known something like this would happen.

"Of all people, Kate, you should know what Karl
is capable of."

"You were right, Tyler. I should have let you
handle this."

"I'm not interested in being right," he said, sympathy in his voice now. "I'd just like to see you permanently free of that slime bag."

"They teach you those words at Yale?" she asked, aware that this was as close as she'd ever heard Tyler get to being angry.

"I could think of some better ones," he said. "And how did Cole handle having his boat stolen?"

"He didn't take it very well."

"I can imagine."

"I don't care about the money, Tyler," she said, running a hand through her hair and watching Louis dig in the sand around the terrace outside the room. "He can have it."

"Not if I have anything to do with it," Tyler said. "Give me all the information you have about who's looking for the boat. I'd like to speak to the authorities about what should happen to that money if they find it."

"Knowing Karl, he'll have buried it at sea," she said. She told him then what little she knew, adding that she wasn't sure when she would be back. She hung up, aware that she had made a complete wreck of things.

Louis came back into the room and sat down on the bed beside her. "Don't be sad, Kate," he said. "You didn't do anything wrong."

She wished it could be that simple. That a mistake could be rectified with a plea for forgiveness. "But I did, Louis."

"That doesn't make you a bad person," he said, sounding much older than the boy she'd watched playing in the sand a few minutes before.

She put her arm around his shoulders, pulling him close and resting her chin on the top of his head.

"Mr. Dillon said once you've said you're sorry, the mistake goes away. It's what you do to make up for it that matters."

She closed her eyes and felt a single tear slide down her cheek. Louis was right. She would not look at what had happened today as an ending. But as a beginning. From here, she had somewhere to go.

MARGO'S FATHER CALLED her room at just after five to say he was having dinner with Lyle and Lily. The strange part was that he didn't invite her to join them. Not sure what to make of it, she hung up the phone and wondered if she should go check on him. But someone knocked on the door just then, and she answered it to find Harry standing there with an ice bucket and two glasses in his hand.

"Someone ordered champagne?"

She shook her head and said, "You must have the wrong room, sir."

"Oh, but the kitchen said it would be the room with the good-looking brunette."

"It's pitiful how susceptible I am to your flattery."

"Handy, too," he said, stepping past her and setting the glasses on a nearby table. "Would you like to open it, or shall I?"

"Oh, do go ahead," she said.

He loosened the wire and then aimed the cork at the ceiling. A single push, and it bounced off the slow-twirling fan, missing her left eye by a hair's breadth on its way back to the floor. "I didn't say I was an expert," he said.

"Obviously."

"So I'll take you to dinner to make up for it."

"Aren't you the gentleman who lost his wallet?"

"I have impeccable credit."

"Taste, as well, I see," she said, glancing at the French label.

"I aim to impress."

He filled a glass and passed it to her, then poured one for himself. He raised it and said, "A toast?"

She lifted hers and waited.

"To nontraditional vacations. And the very interesting people you meet on them."

They clinked the rims of their glasses and took a sip. "Mmm," she said. "And I didn't think I liked champagne."

"There's more where this came from."

"Am I sensing an ulterior motive here?"

"I could take the more direct approach, if you'd prefer," he said, one eyebrow wiggling in a theatrical gesture.

"And where would this direct approach be heading?" she asked, her voice suggestive in a way that definitely wasn't her.

He studied her for a few moments, suddenly serious. "I guess that would depend on where you want to go."

She felt sure Harry had been places she'd never even thought to imagine. She had the sensation of having stepped in quicksand, only to realize it was too late to pull herself out. Her pulse began an insistent thump, and even though she knew there was nothing remotely intelligent in the decision, she wanted to go wherever he led her.

He stepped forward, taking her glass and placing it next to his. He touched her face, smoothed the back of his hand across her hair. The look in his eyes said everything she'd never imagined a man like Harry saying to her.

He found some music on the radio, then pulled

her into his arms and waltzed her around the room. And it was as if all of it happened in slow motion. She wanted it to last as long as it possibly could.

They danced a half dozen or so songs, coming to an easy stop alongside the bed. They were both flushed and smiling, and she thought how nice it was that they had fun together. Something she'd actually known very little of. Maybe that was what drew her to him. Made her wilt under the heat of his kiss. Or it could just be that he was exceptionally good at kissing.

The bed was soft and welcoming beneath them. Their clothes ended up in a pile on the floor, and she couldn't help taking a long look at this man she could not seem to resist.

"I trust everything meets with your approval, ma'am," he said in a teasing voice.

"Oh, I think so," she said, trying not to smile.

"Just making sure." He laughed and then kissed her again. "I'd sure hate to disappoint."

Somehow, she knew there was little chance of that. As it turned out, she was right. And eventually, they finished the champagne. But they never did make it to dinner.

CHAPTER SEVENTEEN

The wounds of love can only be healed by the one who made them.—Publilius Syrus

THE ADDRESS SAM had given Cole at the Atlanta airport just over an hour before was on the outskirts of a wealthy Buckhead Street. He parked the rental car in the driveway, got out and made himself walk to the door when what he wanted to do was run. He imagined Pamela spotting him from an upstairs window and escaping out a back door.

He rang the doorbell, its deep-throated rumble echoing his pounding heart. In a few moments, the door opened, and Pamela stood before him, her expression completely neutral of surprise, as if she'd been expecting him. She'd cut her hair, and it was darker now. She appeared thinner, too, as if these past two years had not come without a price.

"Hello, Cole," she said. "Come in."

He stood for a moment, too surprised by her

calm greeting to respond. He forced his feet to move and followed her into the foyer and across a hall to a large living room that looked out over a vast green yard. It was the kind of room that echoed when you walked, big enough to park a tractor trailer in, the kind of living room found in houses featured in *Architectural Digest*.

Pamela stopped in front of a cavernous fireplace, motioning for him to sit.

He ignored the invitation and got to the point, pushing back the anger hovering just beneath the surface of his control. "I want to see Ginny. Where is she?"

"Upstairs," she said.

"Would you like to get her or should I?" he asked.

"Can you wait a moment?" She asked the question with even-toned politeness.

"I've waited two years," he said, his tone abrupt.

"I knew you'd find us eventually."

The anger blasted up then, coloring his response red. "So was this some kind of game to you?"

"It was never a game," she said.

"What was it then?"

She sighed, ran a hand through her hair. "When I first left with Ginny, I was just plain pissed off at you, Cole."

"Did taking my daughter away from me satisfy your need for revenge?"

She actually winced a little at the question. "I didn't intend to keep her from you for long, but after I started to make a new life for myself, it just seemed easier to make a clean break."

Cole stared at her, not sure if he could even find the words to respond. "Easier for me? Easier for Ginny? Or just easier for you?"

Pamela glanced away, something that might actually have been shame shadowing her eyes. "I think maybe I thought for all of us."

"Well, that's where you were wrong."

She folded her arms across her chest and met his gaze head on. "Why didn't you ever get the police involved?"

"One reason, and one reason only. Believe it or not, I never wanted to destroy my daughter's belief in her mother. What did you tell her, Pamela? Where does she think I've been the last two years?"

Pamela looked down and then met his gaze again before saying, "I told her you didn't have room in your life for us. Was that so very far off the mark?"

In that moment, Cole thought he could understand how people found themselves doing things they would never have thought themselves capable of. He took a step back, counted to five. "Whatever you found me guilty of, and maybe it was all true, I never deserved what you did, Pamela. You stole two years of my daughter's life from me. Two years neither of us can ever get back." He pulled his cell phone from his pocket and flipped it open. "This is what's going to happen. You're going to bring Ginny downstairs and tell her the truth. If you don't, I will call the police, and I will tell them how you kidnapped my daughter in violation of our visitation agreement."

"Cole—"

"This isn't negotiable," he said, the words hard.

"What if she hates me for it?" she asked tentatively.

"You mean the way she's probably hated me?"

Pamela shook her head, started to say something, then pressed her lips together once before conceding. "I'll be right back."

He waited, pacing and nervous. Would Ginny even want to see him? Could he blame her if she didn't?

A minute later, he heard footsteps on the stairs, picking up speed as they got closer.

His daughter burst into the living room, her blond hair long now. She was taller, too, and he felt a knot of emotion in his throat he couldn't seem to swallow back.

"Hi, Ginny, baby," he said, his voice wavering.

"Daddy," she said, tears filling her eyes. "Oh, Daddy, you came back." And then, sobbing, she ran into his open arms.

THROUGH THE HOTEL, Kate arranged for a taxi to pick Louis and her up the next morning and drive them to the orphanage. The air was warm and humid, not a single cloud in the bright blue sky.

Louis sat close to her side, his head on her shoulder. She knew he was sad, and she wasn't sure how she would be able to make herself leave him there.

The ride grew bumpier as they got closer, and Louis was somber when they finally pulled up in front of the worn old building. Kate asked the driver to wait, getting out of the car and walking with Louis across the yard to where Scott stood by the gate.

Louis dropped his gaze, as if afraid he'd be in trouble for what he'd done, but Scott pulled him into his arms and gave him a warm hug and a pat on the back. "I'm glad you're okay, son," he said.

Louis nodded, fighting back tears. Her own eyes stung, and she could barely speak around the lump in her throat. "He's a wonderful boy," she said, looking at Scott.

Scott nodded. "Yes, he is. Thank you for bringing him back safe."

"It was my pleasure."

Louis turned out of Scott's arms to face her. She dropped onto her knees in front of him and took his hands in hers. "I'd like to come back and see you, if that's okay."

He studied her with his wide brown eyes for a few moments, as if unsure she really meant it. He nodded then and said, "I'd like that."

"It's a deal." She pulled him close and hugged him hard, not bothering to hide the tears now streaming down her face. She didn't say any more because she didn't know when she would be back. She just knew that she would. She gave him one last hug, then jumped up and ran back to the taxi.

She looked back once as the old car pulled away in a groan of rattles and a cloud of exhaust. Louis waved. She lifted her hand just before he disappeared from sight.

SHE ARRIVED BACK at the hotel to find the Granger sisters out front waiting for a taxi to take them into town.

"How are you, my dear?" they asked in unison at the sight of her tear-streaked face.

"I just took Louis back to the orphanage."

They each put an arm around her, enfolding her in a sympathetic embrace, patting her back as devoted grandmothers would.

"What a sweet boy he is," Lyle said.

"He really seemed taken with you," Lily added.

"Couldn't you adopt him?" Lyle asked.

Kate pulled back, wiping her face. "I don't think I'm in a position to do something like that," she said. "My life is kind of a wreck right now."

"Maybe he'd be just the thing to fix you up," Lily said. "I have no doubt you'd be good for him."

Lyle took Kate's hand and looked her in the eyes. "When you get as old as I am, there's one thing you'll know for sure. And that is this. The only things that end up being of any value at all are the things you never thought you could do, but did anyway. The rest of it really won't matter."

She nodded, not trusting herself to speak. It was amazing to her that after everything that had happened, they could still see her as someone deserving of something as wonderful as Louis.

She hugged them again and told them she would be leaving later that afternoon. She'd spoken to Tyler early that morning and he'd had his secretary book a flight for her from Tango Island to the Dominican Republic and then on to Miami where she'd left her car.

They promised to keep in touch, exchanging phone numbers and addresses. She stood and watched until they were out of sight, already feeling a pang of loss for the dear friends she'd made on this trip.

"Kate!"

She turned to find Margo waving from the main entrance of the hotel. They agreed to go for a drink on the veranda, both of them ordering a glass of iced tea.

Kate only had to look at Margo to know things with Harry had progressed to a new level. "You're glowing," she said.

Color highlighted Margo's cheeks. "It's that obvious?"

"I'm happy for you," she said. "I can't deny that I'm a little envious, too."

"I don't see how anything permanent can come of it," she said, tracing a pattern through the condensation on her glass.

"Would you like for it to?"

"I haven't let myself consider it."

"Why?"

"My life is complicated. I care about my father—"

"And he obviously cares about you. Surely, he wants to see you happy."

"Harry lives on a yacht in the Caribbean. I live in Massachusetts. How could that ever work?"

"If something is real, it will find a way."

"I guess that's the part I'm not sure about." She was quiet for a moment, before saying, "What about you, Kate? You and Cole were—"

"That's done."

She reached over, put her hand on Kate's. "Are you sure?"

Kate shook her head, trying to smile. "Some fences can't be mended. I'm pretty certain this is one of them."

Harry appeared at the other end of the veranda, waving and walking their way. He leaned down and kissed Margo on the cheek. He took her hand in his, and Kate could see Margo was pleased by his chivalry.

"Just got word," he said. "They've found the boat. Your ex-husband and his helper are being held in the local jail."

At this news, Kate wasn't sure what she should feel. A little over a week ago, she would have felt all sorts of glee. Now, it was more like sadness for the mess she'd made of her life. Karl's incarceration was simply glaring proof of it. "You'll get all of your things back?" she asked.

"I'm headed down to see about it now. You girls want to go with me?"

They both agreed, and the three of them caught a taxi to the pier. The boat sat tied up alongside a dock, and just the sight of it made her think of Cole. Tears stung the back of her eyes, and she felt overwhelmed by a sinking sense of loss.

Harry had to get permission for them to go on board where they were allowed to get their belongings. She let herself into her cabin, not surprised to find that her suitcase had been ransacked, her clothes strewn across the floor. She picked everything up one piece at a time and repacked, closing the latches of the bag with a final-sounding click.

The leather satchel that held the money she'd taken back from Karl was nowhere in sight. She left the room without bothering to look for it.

IT WAS PROBABLY a bad idea, but she needed to see him.

Harry and Margo went with her into town where the tiny island jail was located. She'd asked them not to, but they wouldn't hear of it. And once she stood at the front door, aware that Karl was somewhere on the other side, she was glad they'd insisted.

Inside, she gave her name and asked permission to see him. They waited for nearly a half hour before someone came out and directed her through a heavy metal door and down a narrow hallway.

There were four cells on either side of the hall, and Karl's was at the very end on the right. He sat on a narrow cot, elbows on his knees, looking down at the dingy floor beneath his feet.

Kate's escort turned and walked back down the hall. Karl looked up then, his mouth contorted into something closer to a sneer than a smile. "I wondered if you'd come by for a look."

She started to deny the accusation, but then realized it might be true. "How did you find us today?"

"Miracle of modern technology. A little thing called a tracking device."

"Why didn't you just break into my room at the hotel? You've had plenty of opportunities."

"Too bad I couldn't consult with you on the proper break-in plan. You are, after all, the expert."

"How could you do this, Karl?" she asked.

"You mean take advantage of you," he said, his voice layered with disbelief. "How could I not? You were such an easy target. If it hadn't been me, it would have been someone else."

The words hit her like a knife in the chest. And maybe their power lay in the mere fact that she could not deny their truth. Shame flooded through her, dousing any anger she might have still been harboring for her ex-husband. "You're right," she said. "I was."

His eyes widened, the smirk on his lips faltering.

"What? Are you all done with the revenge theme now?"

She stared at him for several long seconds, long enough for him to shift a little awkwardly on the cot. "As a matter of fact, I am," she said. "Completely done."

She backed up a step, then turned and headed back the way she'd come.

"Kate," he called out. "Wait! You need to get me out of here!"

"Call Tiffany," she said. And she kept walking. Feeling lighter with every step.

BACK AT THE hotel, Kate said she was going to her room to pack up a few things. Harry and Margo lingered out front, a little awkward now that they were alone again. He took her hand and led her to a bench under a stand of palm trees. They sat for a few moments before either of them spoke, and then it was at the same time.

"I think we should talk about—" he began.

"Dad and I are leaving—"

They both broke off, staring at one another in silence.

"Leaving when?" he finally asked.

"This afternoon," she said. "There's a five o'clock flight to San Juan."

"This afternoon," he repeated. "But what about—"

"Harry," she said. "Last night was lovely, but we both knew it couldn't outlive this vacation."

He had to admit he was a little stunned by this. He thought of all the times he'd been the one bowing out, making excuses. He'd never imagined how it felt to be on the receiving end of it. "Is this about your father?" he asked. "Do you think he won't approve?"

"It's not that simple."

"Well, see, I think it is. You can't leave, Margo. We just found each other."

The words swayed her. He could see it in her eyes. But he also saw the conflict there, and he somehow knew he wasn't going to win this one.

She stood, pressing a hand to his cheek, then bending down and kissing him. He tasted the sweetness of their night together on her lips, and he could honestly say he'd been changed by it. "'Bye, Harry," she said and walked away.

"Margo. Wait!"

But she just walked faster until she was running, and he was once again alone.

HARRY SAT FOR a long time after she'd gone. Just thinking.

For a lot of years now, he'd been the one with

the trust issues. His life had been what he'd made it. No commitment. Just fun and games. And that's how he'd wanted it.

Until now. Until Margo. And he felt as if he'd walked into a wall. Suddenly, his eyes were opened to the truth of his life and its hollow emptiness. He realized that without her, he would be lonely in a way he'd never imagined he could be.

He wondered how a thirty-five-year-old woman could turn him down because her father disapproved of him. He considered this for a good bit, coming at it from every angle he could come up with. Until it hit him that it wasn't her father's approval that she needed. It was something else entirely. She needed to know that he believed she would be safe. That the man she was with would do everything in his power to take care of her.

Without a single doubt in his mind, Harry knew he was that man. Somehow, he needed to prove it first to Dr. Sheldon and then to Margo.

THE PLANE THAT took Kate to the Dominican Republic was small and noisy. There were only four other passengers on the flight, and she sat with her eyes closed, trying not to notice the bumps.

She did a cowardly thing and left a note for Margo and Harry. She just couldn't bring herself to say goodbye in person. Leaving them felt like another loss, and she'd rather leave it open-ended with the possibility that they would see each other again.

Maybe she'd hung on to this because of how things ended with Cole. Because that loss *was* real.

She looked out the window, still able to spot Tango Island in the distance. She knew without a doubt that her life had changed on that island. There, she'd fallen in love with a man who made her want to be a better version of herself. Who, she realized now, would never know whether she'd managed to get it right or not.

She thought of Louis, too, and the look in his eyes when she'd left him at the orphanage. *Couldn't you adopt him?* Lyle's question came floating back to her. It had seemed preposterous at the time, but she wondered now at her reasons for dismissing it so easily. Selfishness? Inconvenience?

To her credit, she didn't think so. Adoption seemed like something worthy of a more responsible person than she'd been, someone who had made better life choices. But then, wasn't that the person she wanted to be from this point forward? And if she kept looking back at her past, how would she ever move on to a future?

With a quiet conviction, she suddenly knew what she wanted one of the first steps in this new life to be. She needed Louis as much as he needed her. What better reason was there?

She watched as Tango Island became smaller and smaller, until it was a speck in the distance and then gone altogether. Only then did she turn around and face forward, content in knowing she would be back.

AT THREE O'CLOCK, Margo followed a porter to the lobby with her suitcases. She'd been trying to call Kate's room for the last hour and still hadn't reached her. At the front desk, she asked if Kate was still in the hotel, only to learn that she'd already checked out. Margo couldn't believe that Kate would have left without saying goodbye. She was still trying to figure out what to make of this when another young woman behind the counter handed her an envelope.

"Your father asked that I make sure you receive this," she said with a smile.

Margo glanced around the lobby, expecting to see him. He was nowhere in sight so she opened it and pulled out a letter written on the hotel's stationery. She read the first line, her eyes speeding across the words.

My dearest Margo,
I would hope by now, despite my often clumsy methods of showing it, that you know

how very much I love you. I think it's sometimes difficult to take a step back and look at
our own actions with an objective eye. Since
the day you walked back into my arms after
I had come to think I would never see you
again, I have tried to hold on to you, terrified,
I guess, that you might disappear as you had
before. I hope you will look at my motivation
rather than my mistakes, though I know there
have been plenty. There's been a destination
for us both on this trip. Mine to the realization that what I really want is to see you happy
and fulfilled. Now you just need to figure out
what yours has been.

Love,

Daddy

With those last two words, a sob rose out of her
chest. She pressed her hand to her mouth, crossing
the lobby to sit on a wide leather chair where she
read the note over again.

"Hey."

She looked up to find Harry standing in front of
her, his hands shoved in his pockets like a little boy
unsure of his reception. "Do you know anything
about this?" she asked.

"He wants you to be happy, hon," Harry said, his voice soft.

"What did you say to him?"

"That I want to be the man responsible for your happiness."

Fresh tears welled in her eyes, and she let them fall, not bothering to wipe them away. "Harry. Be realistic. How could this ever work?"

He sat down next to her, took her hands in his. "Seems to me that it starts with the two of us wanting it to. From there, all options are open."

Before her sat a man she would never have imagined herself with. He had lived a life that could not be more opposite from hers. But did that negate the possibility that they could merge the two? There was no doubt that such an attempt would be a leap of faith. She had no idea if there was a bottom below. But she wanted to find out. And so she reached for his hand and jumped.

COLE AND GINNY arrived in Miami just before six o'clock. On the flight from Atlanta, she'd entertained him with games of old maid and go fish. It amazed him that they could have been apart for this long and pick up where they'd left off, father and daughter. Only he realized that wasn't exactly true.

Two years ago, he wouldn't have had time for a game of cards. Or rather, he wouldn't have made time for it. There was the difference. And he was unspeakably grateful that he now had another chance to get this right.

Angry as he had been with Pamela, it had been painful to listen as she'd tried to explain her actions to their daughter. When she'd finally run out of words and lapsed into a stilted silence, Ginny had sat quietly, studying her mother for several long moments before saying, "I wish you hadn't done that, Mama. I thought Daddy didn't love me anymore."

That was the stake through Cole's heart, and if it hadn't been for his own agony, he might have actually felt sorry for Pamela. Regret clouding her eyes, she'd reached for Ginny's hand, only to shrink back when the child refused to let her touch her.

Cole had no desire to stoke resentment in his daughter, but he did understand that she would need time to work through her feelings on everything that had happened. And he intended to give her that time.

On the way to the rental car parking lot, he called Harry. He'd spoken to him earlier, letting him know that he and Pamela had reached an agreement on how they would divide Ginny's time between them and that he was heading back to Tango Island to get the boat. He wanted to show his daughter where he'd been the past couple of years. The hotel put him through to Harry's room, and Cole barely recognized his friend's voice when he answered.

"Are you underwater?" he asked.

Harry cleared his throat and said, "Not exactly."

"You sound all choked up."

"To tell you the truth I was in the middle of telling the woman I love how much I want to marry her."

It took a moment for this to settle, and then Cole said, "You were what?"

"You heard right," Harry said, a smile in his voice now.

"Wonders never cease. Margo, I presume?"

"Yep. And you know what's even more amazing?"

"What could be more amazing than that?"

"She said yes."

"That is even more amazing."

"Aw, come on, now. Congratulations are in order!"

"You're right," he said, smiling now. "They certainly are. Congratulations, old man. I never thought I'd see the day."

"It's all about finding the right woman."

"Oh, now you're an expert on the subject."

"You can't deny my success."

"No, I can't."

"You've had a little success of your own, you know."

Cole didn't have to ask. He knew Harry was talking about Kate.

"She left this afternoon. In fact, she ought to be getting into Miami any time now. She was flying out of the Dominican Republic."

"Yeah, thanks, Harry."

"You're not going to hold the boat thing against her, are you? Because if you do, it's just—"

"Harry. Let me speak to Margo."

After a series of rustling sounds, Margo said hello.

"I take it you know what you're getting into."

"I have a bit of an idea," she said, then giggled and told Harry to keep his hands to himself.

"He's a good man, Margo."

"I know," she said. "And Cole?"

"Yeah?"

"Kate's a good woman."

"I've gotta go," he said, too quickly, "but I'll see you guys tomorrow. Ginny will be with me."

"I can't wait to meet her."

They hung up then, and Ginny passed him a piece of construction paper on which she had drawn a family of bunny rabbits. The daddy rabbit had really big ears. The mama rabbit had extra little feet. And the babies had noses that were a little too long for their faces. "It's beautiful, honey," he said. "Thank you."

"They look kind of funny," Ginny said, but he could see that she was proud he liked it. And he did. Looking at his daughter's picture, he realized that something didn't have to be perfect to be irreplaceable.

He glanced at his watch as the bus pulled to a stop in front of the rental office. He took Ginny's hand and led her down the steps. "There's someone else I know who apparently has a talent for drawing. If we hurry, I think we can catch her. I'd really like for you to meet her."

THE PLANE TOUCHED down in Miami at just after six-thirty. Kate followed the line of passengers through the corridor into the main terminal, trying not to notice the hugs and kisses awaiting each of them.

She lowered her head and threaded her way through the throng, picking up her pace as she reached the edge of the crowd.

"Kate!"

The voice stopped her cold, and she stood for a moment, certain she'd imagined it.

"Kate."

This time, she turned, and there he was. Cole. Looking at her with those incredible blue eyes. A beautiful little girl standing next to him, her hand clasped in his. He walked closer, stopping in front of her.

"This is my daughter, Ginny," he said. "Ginny, this is the lady I told you about. The one who likes to draw."

"Hi," she said, her voice soft and sweet, shyness making her drop her gaze.

"Hi, Ginny," she replied, her throat suddenly tight. "What do you like to draw?"

"Rabbits."

"I like rabbits," Kate said.

"She's pretty good," Cole added.

Ginny looked up. "He's my daddy, so he doesn't notice when I mess up, but I mess up a lot."

Neither of them said anything for a few moments, the silence weighted.

"I guess that's what we do when we love someone," Cole said.

Kate felt his gaze on her and forced herself to look at him. Her heart was beating way too fast, and she was suddenly afraid to believe what she'd heard.

"We're going back to Tango Island tomorrow morning to get the boat," he said. "Any chance you'd like to go with us?"

It was the last question she'd expected, and she couldn't find any words to answer him. She wanted to ask him about all the other stuff. Her deception. His understandable disillusion.

But she could see that he had put it all aside. Closed the door.

It couldn't possibly be this simple.

But then, maybe it was.

Maybe when it was real, it was this simple.

"Yeah," she said. "I'd very much like to go with you."

Something she would have to call happiness lit his eyes. He reached down and lifted the handle of her bag. Ginny volunteered to help him pull it. Cole put his arm around her shoulders and leaned in to kiss her temple.

And together, they walked through the airport and out to his car. No directions needed. She'd finally found her true north.

EPILOGUE

Gold is where you find it.—American Proverb

SOMETIMES, IT WAS hard for Kate to believe the way life could change in a single year.

But as she stood just outside the circle of her family and friends, she was grateful for what she now had in a way she couldn't express.

They were back on Tango Island, this time for a two-week working vacation where they were building an addition to the orphanage. Margo and Harry were scrapping over the same hammer, both declaring it the one they'd laid claim to that morning. Margo was six months pregnant, and Harry had actually become one of those husbands who felt all the same things she was feeling. Morning sickness. Back pain. Mood swings. Another one for the talk shows, Margo said. Kate thought it a good example of how love could change a person from the inside out.

And then there was her family. She still had trouble saying the words without a shiver of fear that this happiness might disappear as quickly as it had appeared in her life. Cole stood at the top of the ladder, Ginny hovering at the side and passing him nails one at a time. Louis had his feet planted wide and solid, hands steady at the base of the ladder in his own effort to make sure his daddy didn't fall.

Louis's protectiveness of both her and Cole brought tears to her eyes every time she let herself think about the reasons behind it. The adoption was finally completed two months ago, six months after she and Cole were married in a small island church overlooking the ocean.

Ginny loved having a brother, and Kate still had trouble believing that she'd been given the privilege of having these two amazing children in her life.

Cole hammered the last nail, calling out, "That's it. We're done for the day."

He started down the ladder, and Louis didn't move until he was safely back on the ground. Only then did he and Ginny start jumping up and down, chanting, "We're going to see the dolphins! We're going to see the dolphins!"

Harry and Margo had arranged to take the two of them, along with the children from the orphanage, to a dolphin show on the other side of the island.

Kate and Cole had volunteered to chaperone, but Harry had insisted he and Margo needed the practice.

Ginny and Louis gave them each a hug and a kiss. Then Kate and Cole stood in the dusty driveway, watching as Scott directed the group onto the open-sided bus Harry had rented for the excursion.

They waved as it pulled away, laughter and chatter flowing out behind it. When the bus was out of sight, Cole turned to her, brushing the back of his hand across her cheek. "Ah, we're actually alone," he said.

She cocked her head and listened for a moment. "Silence. It's a little weird, isn't it?"

Cole looked at his watch. "It's only four o'clock. I could think of a thing or two we could do with all this free time."

"Yeah?" She kept her expression serious. "I do have some laundry back at the hotel that needs to be done."

"That's not exactly what I had in mind," he said, a smile touching the corners of his mouth.

"So what were you thinking?"

He steered her backward across the small parking lot until she came to a stop against a leaning palm tree.

"There are a number of things a newly married

couple could do when they actually find themselves alone together."

She raised an eyebrow, pretending to give it consideration. "Checkers? Chinese or regular. I'm not picky."

He gave her a smoky look that never failed to weaken her knees. "I guess there's a version of that I might find interesting."

"What version is that?" she asked, hearing the skip in her voice.

He leaned in then, smelling of wood and hard work, kissing her dirt-smudged neck and undoing the top two buttons of her cotton blouse. "I've been told there's a strip version of checkers that can pass the time."

"Is that so?" she said, slipping her arms around his neck.

"I mean when there's nothing better to do," he added, lifting her hair aside to nibble at her ear.

"You know, a girl could get ideas from a guy like you."

"One could hope," he said, settling his mouth onto hers for a long, ardent kiss.

They indulged themselves as if they had all the time in the world, and when he finally pulled back to look down at her, she melted a little beneath the heat in his eyes.

They walked to the Jeep, and he started it up, then reached across the gear shift for her hand. She leaned her head against the seat, unable to stop herself from smiling.

The sun had begun to drop in the sky, pink melding with blue.

Kate thought of her favorite old movies where the two lovers ride off into the sunset, a clichéd metaphor for a happy ending. She glanced at her husband, now whistling a tune she couldn't quite place. And she didn't mind being a cliché. She had her happy ending.

* * * * *

New York Times *bestselling author*
Linda Lael Miller
is back with a new romance featuring
the heartwarming McKettrick family
from Silhouette Special Edition.

SIERRA'S HOMECOMING
by Linda Lael Miller

On sale December 2006,
wherever books are sold.

Turn the page for a sneak preview!

Soft, smoky music poured into the room.

The next thing she knew, Sierra was in Travis's arms, close against that chest she'd admired earlier, and they were slow dancing.

Why didn't she pull away?

"Relax," he said. His breath was warm in her hair.

She giggled, more nervous than amused. What was the matter with her? She was attracted to Travis, had been from the first, and he was clearly attracted to her. They were both adults. Why not enjoy a little slow dancing in a ranch-house kitchen?

Because slow dancing led to other things. She took a step back and felt the counter flush against her lower back. Travis naturally came with her, since they were holding hands and he had one arm around her waist.

Simple physics.

Then he kissed her.

Physics again—this time, not so simple.

"Yikes," she said, when their mouths parted.

He grinned. "Nobody's ever said that after I kissed them."

She felt the heat and substance of his body pressed against hers. "It's going to happen, isn't it?" she heard herself whisper.

"Yep," Travis answered.

"But not tonight," Sierra said on a sigh.

"Probably not," Travis agreed.

"When, then?"

He chuckled, gave her a slow, nibbling kiss. "Tomorrow morning," he said. "After you drop Liam off at school."

"Isn't that…a little…soon?"

"Not soon enough," Travis answered, his voice husky. "Not nearly soon enough."

nocturne™

**Explore the dark and sensual
new realm of paranormal romance.**

HAUNTED
BY LISA CHILDS

**The first book in the riveting
new 3-book miniseries, Witch Hunt.**

DEATH CALLS
BY CARIDAD PIÑEIRO

**Darkness calls to humans,
as well as vampires...**

*On sale December 2006,
wherever books are sold.*

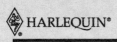
HARLEQUIN®

American ROMANCE®

IS PROUD TO PRESENT

COWBOY VET
by Pamela Britton

Jessie Monroe is the last person on earth
Rand Sheppard wants to rely on, but he needs
a veterinary technician—yesterday—and she's the
only one for hire. It turns out the woman who
destroyed his cousin's life isn't who Rand thought
she was. And now she's all he can think about!

"Pamela Britton writes the kind of
wonderfully romantic, sexy, witty romance
that readers dream of discovering
when they go into a bookstore."

—*New York Times* bestselling author
Jayne Ann Krentz

Cowboy Vet *is available from*
Harlequin American Romance in December 2006.

REQUEST YOUR FREE BOOKS!

2 FREE NOVELS PLUS 2 FREE GIFTS!

HARLEQUIN®

Super Romance®

Exciting, emotional, unexpected!

YES! Please send me 2 FREE Harlequin Superromance® novels and my 2 FREE gifts. After receiving them, if I don't wish to receive any more books, I can return the shipping statement marked "cancel." If I don't cancel, I will receive 6 brand-new novels every month and be billed just $4.69 per book in the U.S., or $5.24 per book in Canada, plus 25¢ shipping and handling per book and applicable taxes, if any*. That's a savings of close to 15% off the cover price! I understand that accepting the 2 free books and gifts places me under no obligation to buy anything. I can always return a shipment and cancel at any time. Even if I never buy another book from Harlequin, the two free books and gifts are mine to keep forever.

135 HDN EEX7   336 HDN EEYK

Name	(PLEASE PRINT)
Address	Apt.
City	State/Prov.	Zip/Postal Code

Signature (if under 18, a parent or guardian must sign)

Mail to Harlequin Reader Service®:

IN U.S.A.	IN CANADA
P.O. Box 1867	P.O. Box 609
Buffalo, NY	Fort Erie, Ontario
14240-1867	L2A 5X3

Not valid to current Harlequin Superromance subscribers.

Want to try two free books from another line?
Call 1-800-873-8635 or visit www.morefreebooks.com.

* Terms and prices subject to change without notice. NY residents add applicable sales tax. Canadian residents will be charged applicable provincial taxes and GST. This offer is limited to one order per household. All orders subject to approval. Credit or debit balances in a customer's account(s) may be offset by any other outstanding balance owed by or to the customer. Please allow 4 to 6 weeks for delivery.

HSR06

Harlequin® Historical
Historical Romantic Adventure!

Loyalty…or love?

LORD GREVILLE'S CAPTIVE
Nicola Cornick

He had previously come to Grafton
Manor to be betrothed to the beautiful
Lady Anne—but that promise was broken
with the onset of the English Civil War.
Now Lord Greville has returned as an
enemy, besieging the manor and holding
its lady prisoner.

His devotion to his cause is swayed by
his desire for Anne—he will have the
lady, and her heart.

Yet Anne has a secret that must be kept
from him at all costs….

On sale December 2006.
Available wherever Harlequin books are sold.

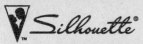

HARLEQUIN®

Romance.

**From the Heart.
For the Heart.**

Get swept away into the Outback
with two of Harlequin Romance's
top authors.

Coming in December...

Claiming the Cattleman's Heart

BY BARBARA HANNAY

And in January don't miss...

Outback Man Seeks Wife

BY MARGARET WAY

Silhouette® Desire

USA TODAY bestselling author

BARBARA McCAULEY

continues her award-winning series

SECRETS!

A NEW BLACKHAWK FAMILY HAS BEEN DISCOVERED... AND THE SCANDALS ARE SET TO FLY!

She touched him once and now Alaina Blackhawk is certain horse rancher DJ Bradshaw will be her first lover. But will the millionaire Texan allow her to leave once he makes her his own?

Blackhawk's Bond

On sale December 2006 (SD #1766)

Available at your favorite retail outlet.

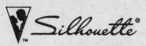